THE ADVENTURES OF

THE BAILEY SCHOOL KIDS

DRAGONS DON'T COOK PIZZA

A GRAPHIC NOVEL BY ANGELI RAFER

BASED ON THE NOVEL BY

MARCIA THORNTON JONES & DEBBIE DADEY

WITH COLOR BY **WES DZIOBA**

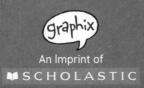

An Imprint of

SCHOLASTIC

TO CONNIE MEYERS: TEACHER, TUTOR, WRITER, AND FRIEND
WHO DELIGHTED IN READING AND WRITING FUN BOOKS FOR
READERS LIKE YOU! — MARCIA THORNTON JONES

TO ALEX — DEBBIE DADEY

TO SARA AND ELISE — MY DEAR FRIENDS, FELLOW STORYTELLERS, DREAMERS, AND
ADVENTURERS. TRULY, YOU TWO ARE THE BEST CONSPIRATORS TO HAVE BY YOUR
SIDE WHEN YOU PLAN TO BURGLE A DRAGON'S DEN — OR TO EMBARK ON SOME
OTHER FANTASTICAL QUEST, LIKE GETTING A BOOK PUBLISHED. — ANGELI RAFER

Text copyright © 1997, 2024 by Marcia Thornton Jones and Debra S. Dadey
Art copyright © 2024 by Angeli Rafer

All rights reserved. Published by Graphix, an imprint of Scholastic Inc., *Publishers since 1920*.
SCHOLASTIC, GRAPHIX, THE ADVENTURES OF THE BAILEY SCHOOL KIDS, and associated logos are
trademarks and/or registered trademarks of Scholastic Inc.

Some character and setting illustrations are either based on or inspired by character and setting
depictions originally designed by Pearl Low.

Library of Congress Control Number: 2023938077

ISBN 978-1-338-88169-1 (hardcover)
ISBN 978-1-338-88168-4 (paperback)

10 9 8 7 6 5 4 3 2 1   24 25 26 27 28

Printed in China   62
First edition, April 2024

Edited by Jonah Newman
Book design by Steve Ponzo and Shivana Sookdeo
Color flatting by Aaron Polk
Creative Director: Phil Falco
Publisher: David Saylor

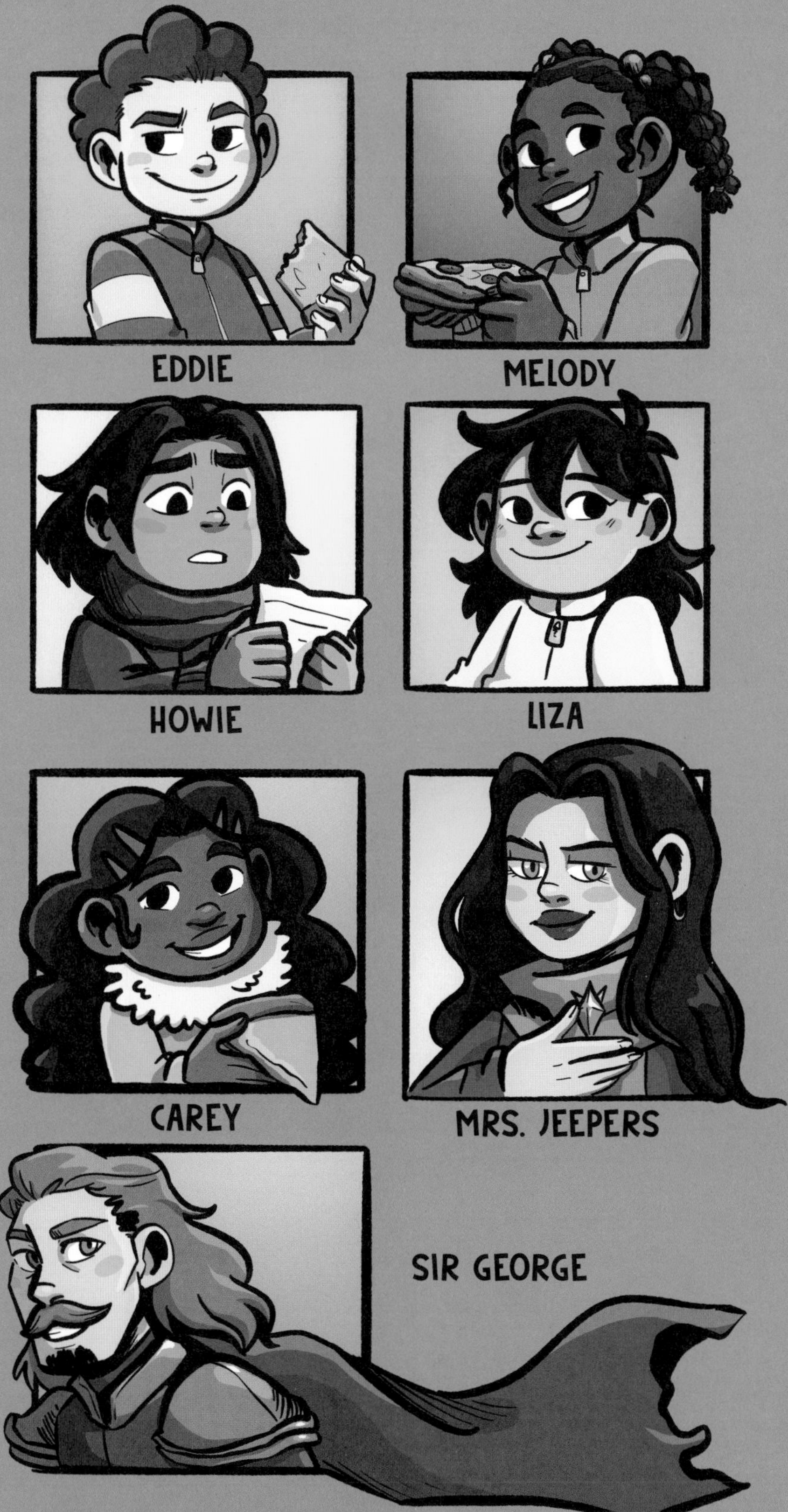
EDDIE
MELODY
HOWIE
LIZA
CAREY
MRS. JEEPERS
SIR GEORGE

CHAPTER 1 JEWEL'S PIZZA CASTLE

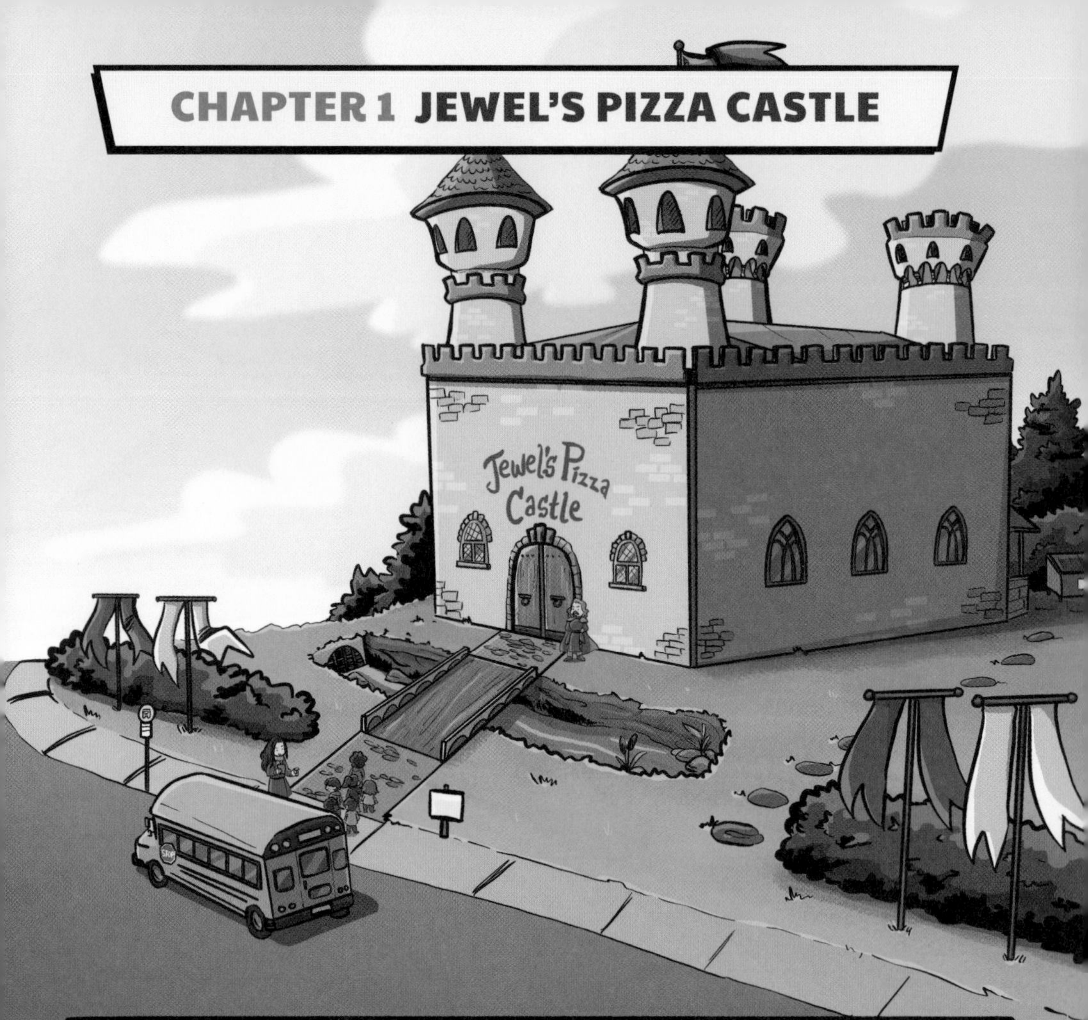
Jewel's Pizza Castle

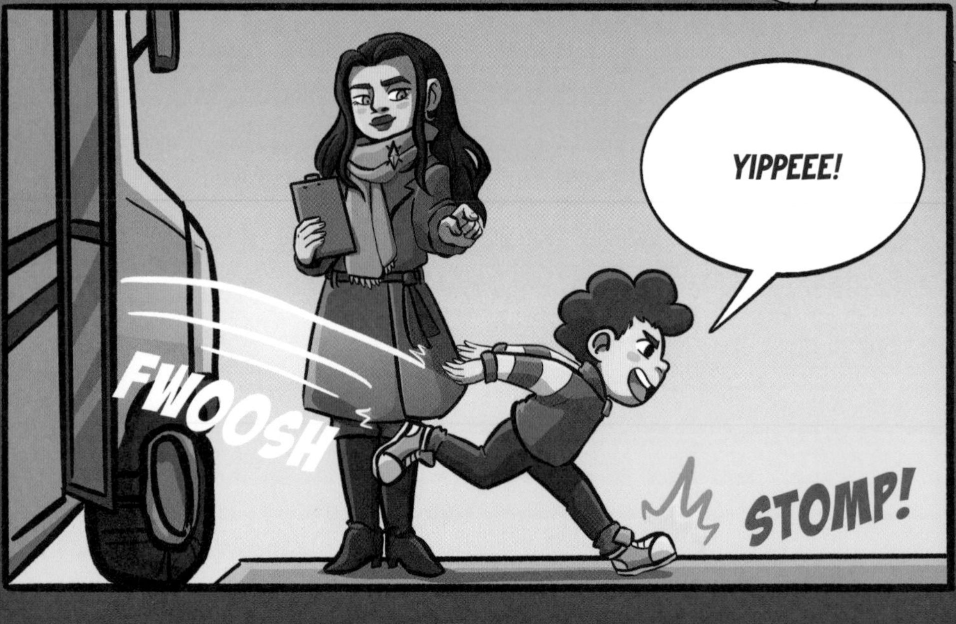
YIPPEEE!
FWOOSH
STOMP!

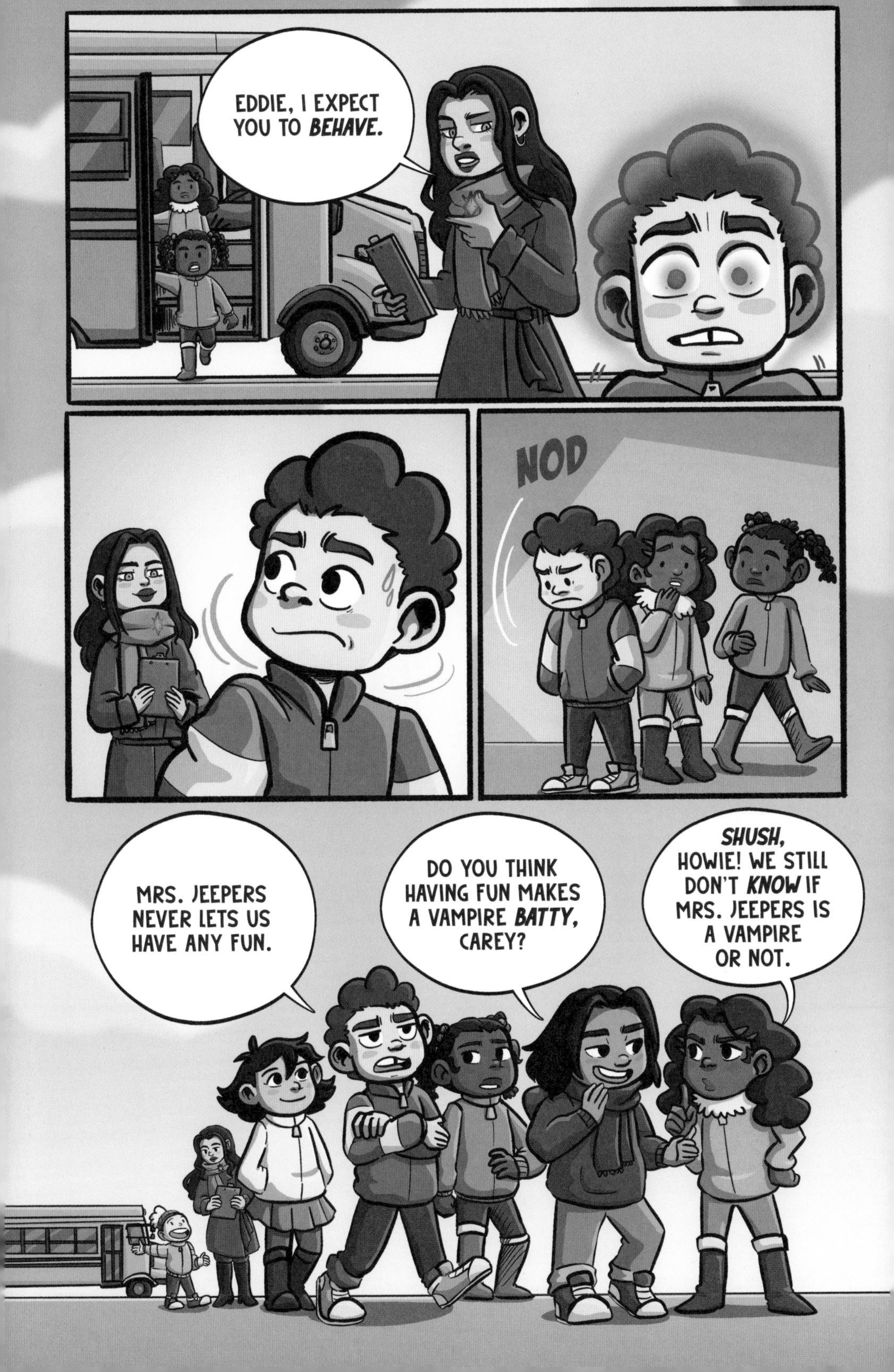
EDDIE, I EXPECT YOU TO BEHAVE.
NOD
MRS. JEEPERS NEVER LETS US HAVE ANY FUN.
DO YOU THINK HAVING FUN MAKES A VAMPIRE BATTY, CAREY?
SHUSH, HOWIE! WE STILL DON'T KNOW IF MRS. JEEPERS IS A VAMPIRE OR NOT.

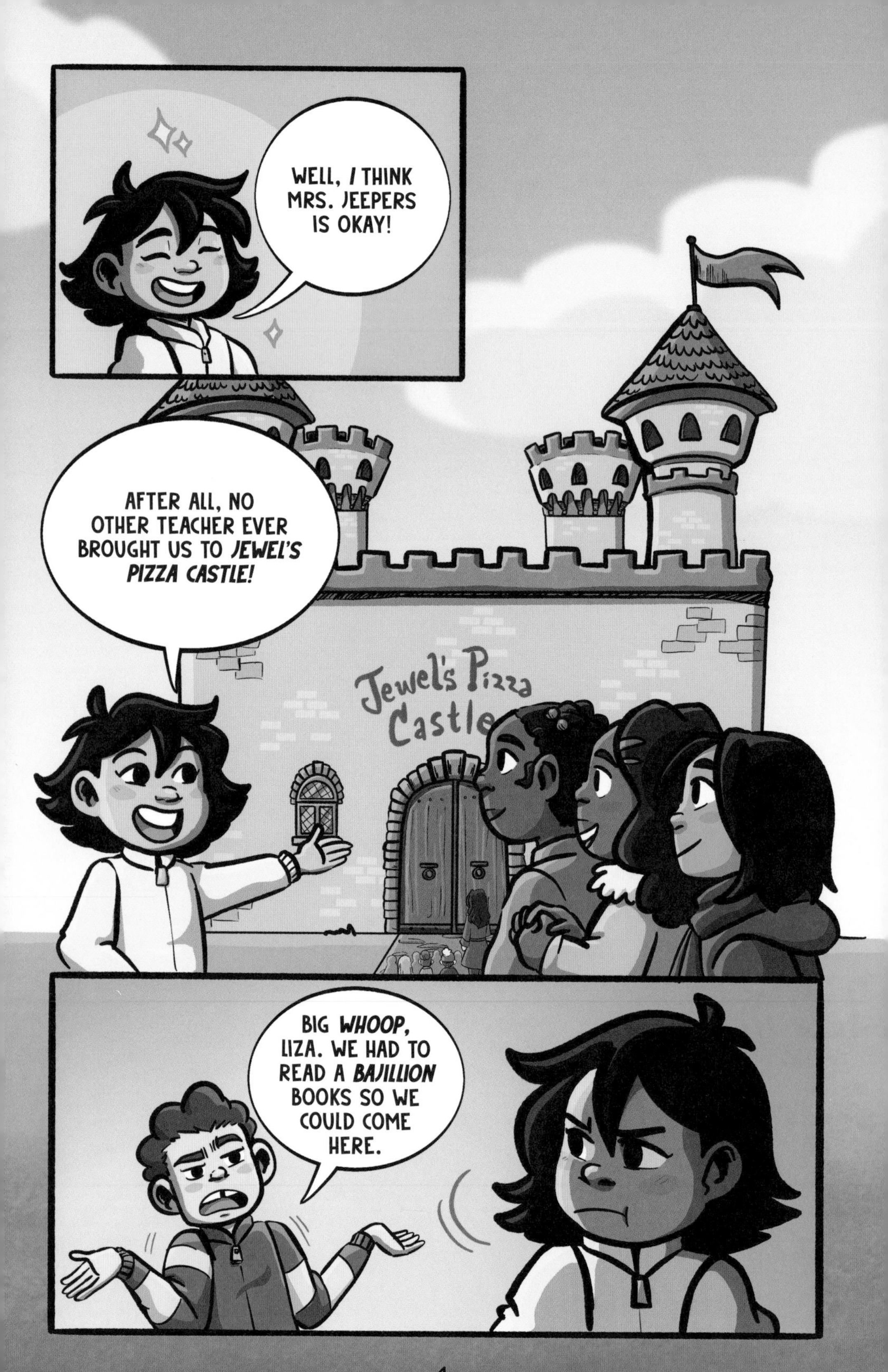

WELL, *I* THINK MRS. JEEPERS IS OKAY!
AFTER ALL, NO OTHER TEACHER EVER BROUGHT US TO *JEWEL'S PIZZA CASTLE!*
Jewel's Pizza Castle
BIG *WHOOP*, LIZA. WE HAD TO READ A *BAJILLION* BOOKS SO WE COULD COME HERE.

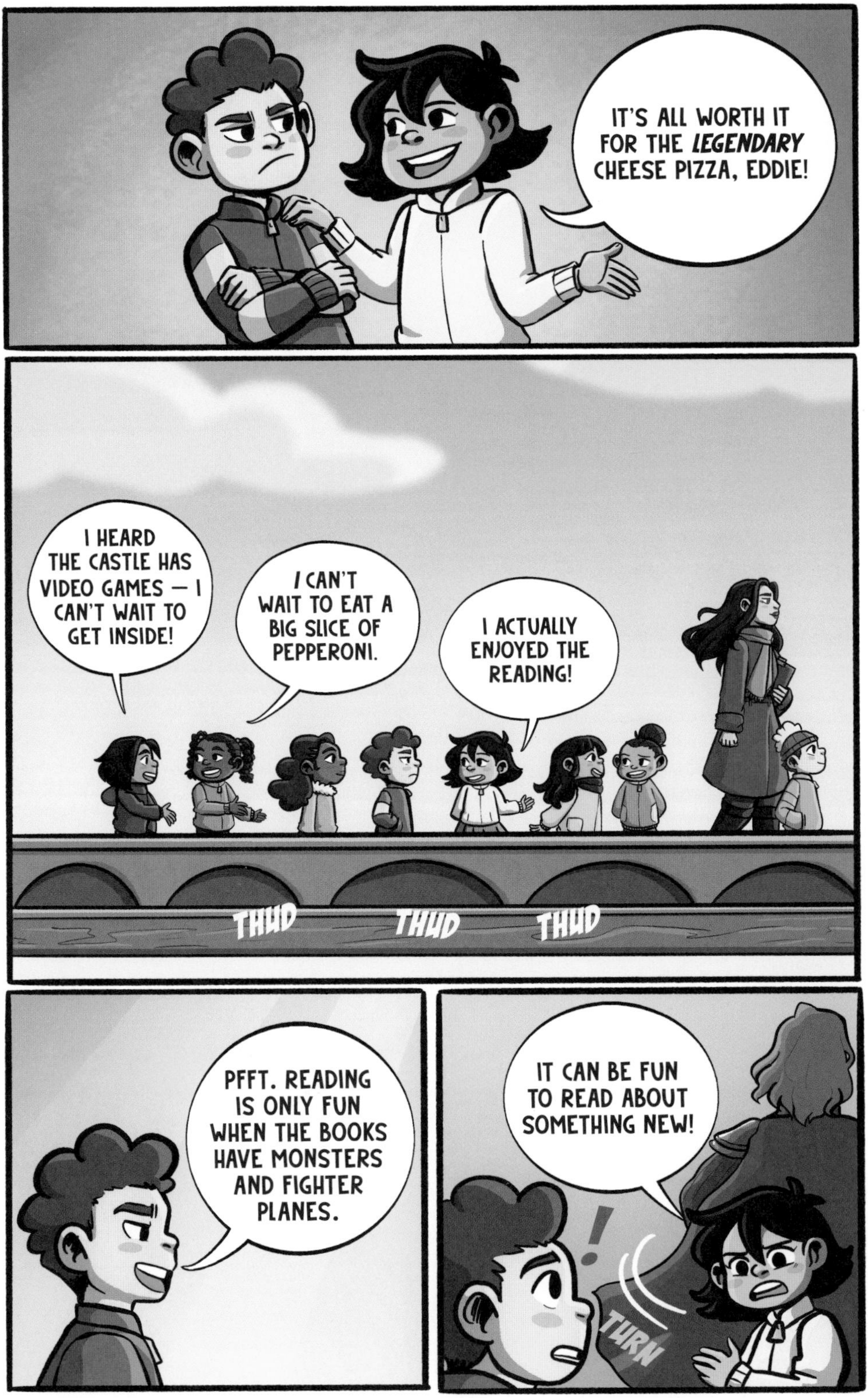
IT'S ALL WORTH IT FOR THE *LEGENDARY* CHEESE PIZZA, EDDIE!
I HEARD THE CASTLE HAS VIDEO GAMES — I CAN'T WAIT TO GET INSIDE!
I CAN'T WAIT TO EAT A BIG SLICE OF PEPPERONI.
I ACTUALLY ENJOYED THE READING!
THUD
THUD
THUD
PFFT. READING IS ONLY FUN WHEN THE BOOKS HAVE MONSTERS AND FIGHTER PLANES.
IT CAN BE FUN TO READ ABOUT SOMETHING NEW!
!
TURN

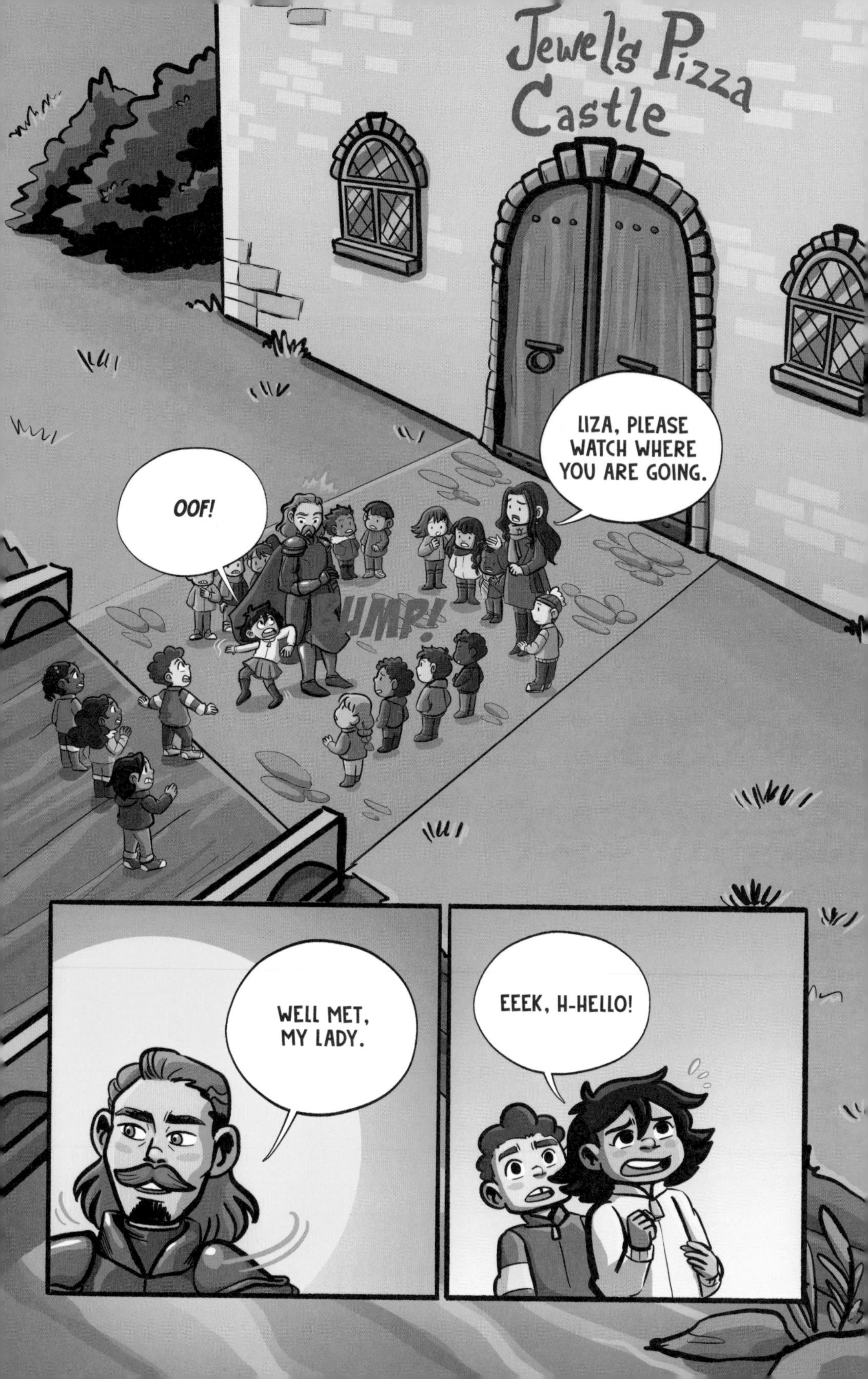
Jewel's Pizza Castle
OOF!
LIZA, PLEASE WATCH WHERE YOU ARE GOING.
WELL MET, MY LADY.
EEEK, H-HELLO!

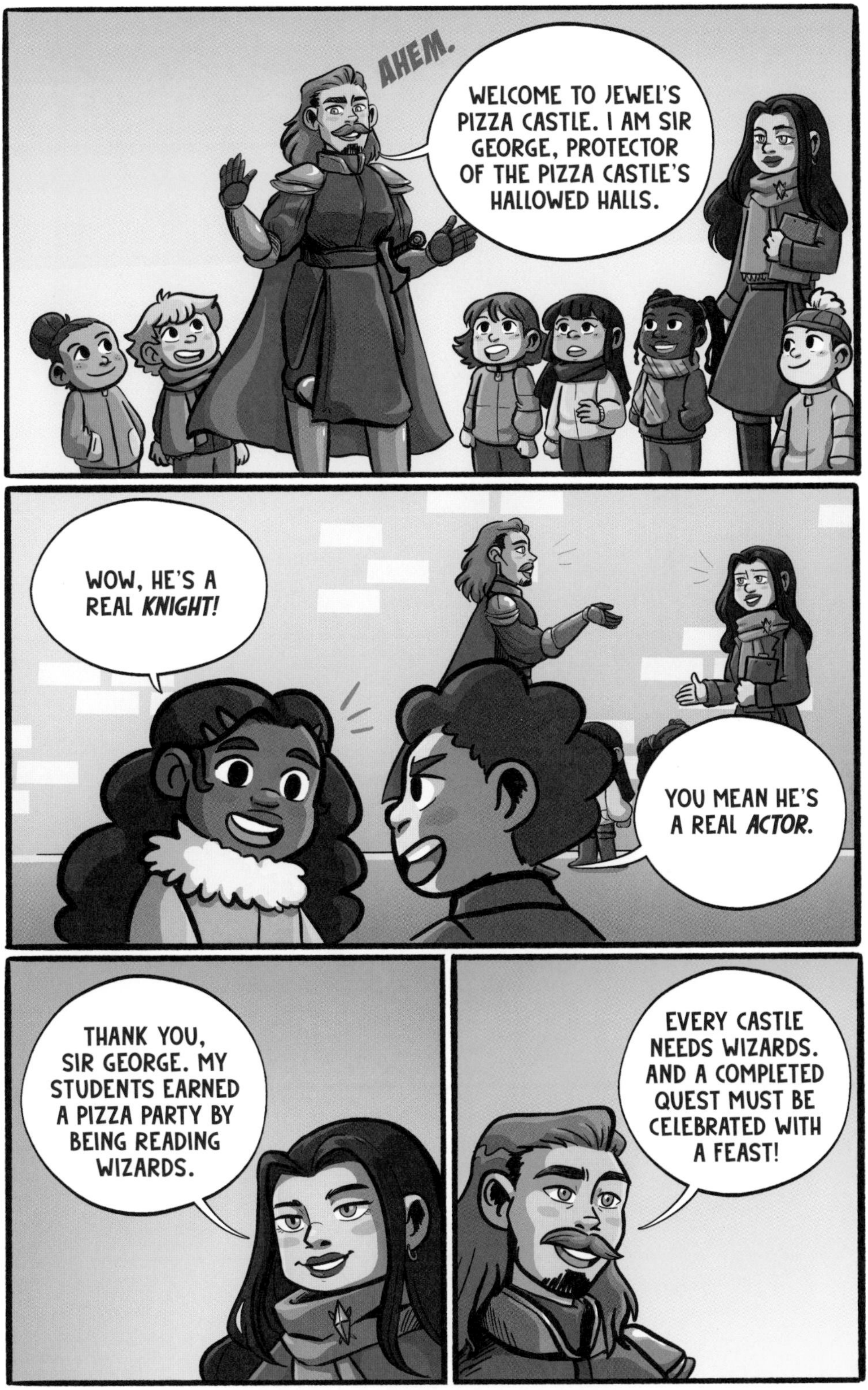
AHEM.
WELCOME TO JEWEL'S PIZZA CASTLE. I AM SIR GEORGE, PROTECTOR OF THE PIZZA CASTLE'S HALLOWED HALLS.
WOW, HE'S A REAL *KNIGHT!*
YOU MEAN HE'S A REAL *ACTOR*.
THANK YOU, SIR GEORGE. MY STUDENTS EARNED A PIZZA PARTY BY BEING READING WIZARDS.
EVERY CASTLE NEEDS WIZARDS. AND A COMPLETED QUEST MUST BE CELEBRATED WITH A FEAST!

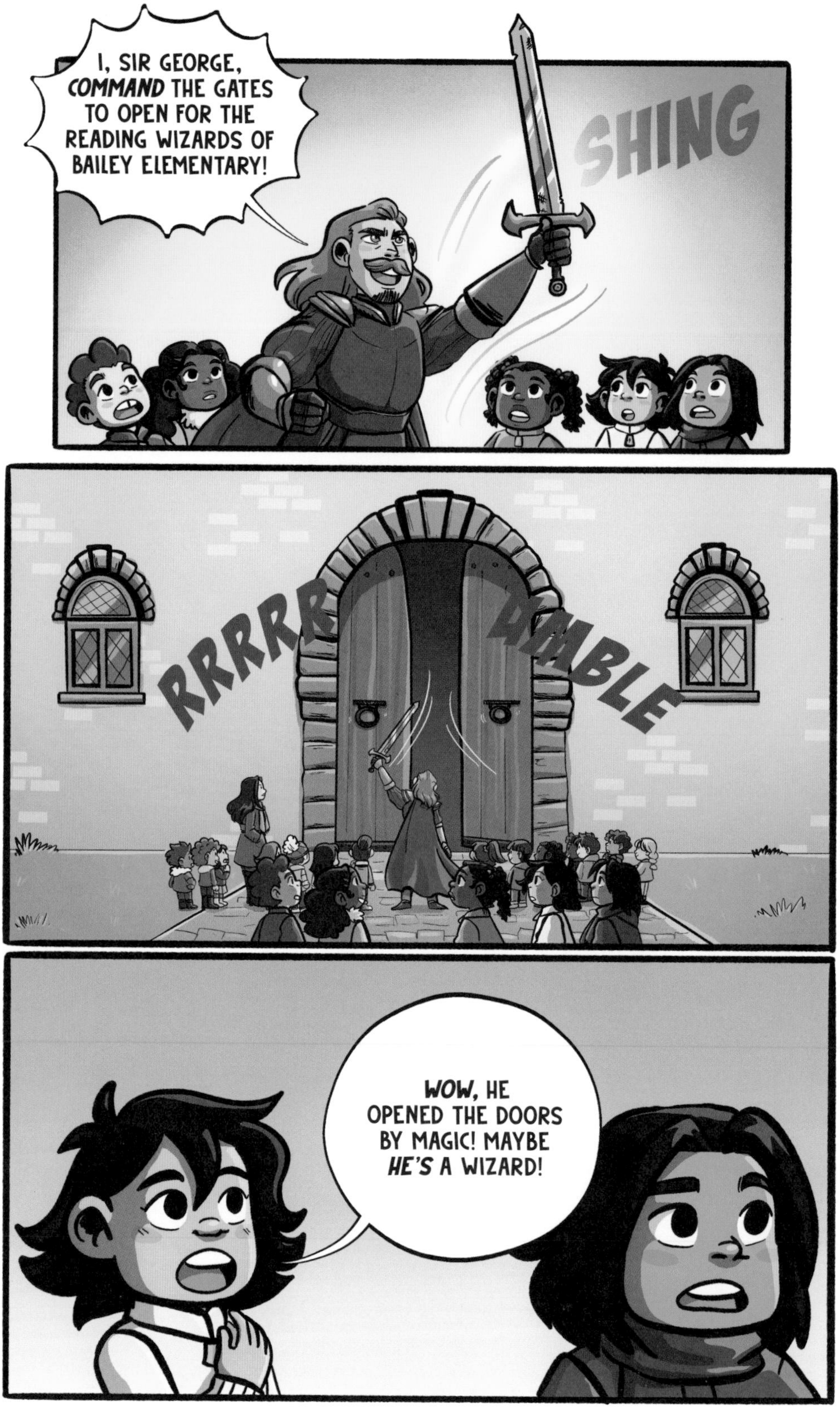
I, SIR GEORGE, COMMAND THE GATES TO OPEN FOR THE READING WIZARDS OF BAILEY ELEMENTARY!
SHING
RRRRRUMBLE
WOW, HE OPENED THE DOORS BY MAGIC! MAYBE HE'S A WIZARD!

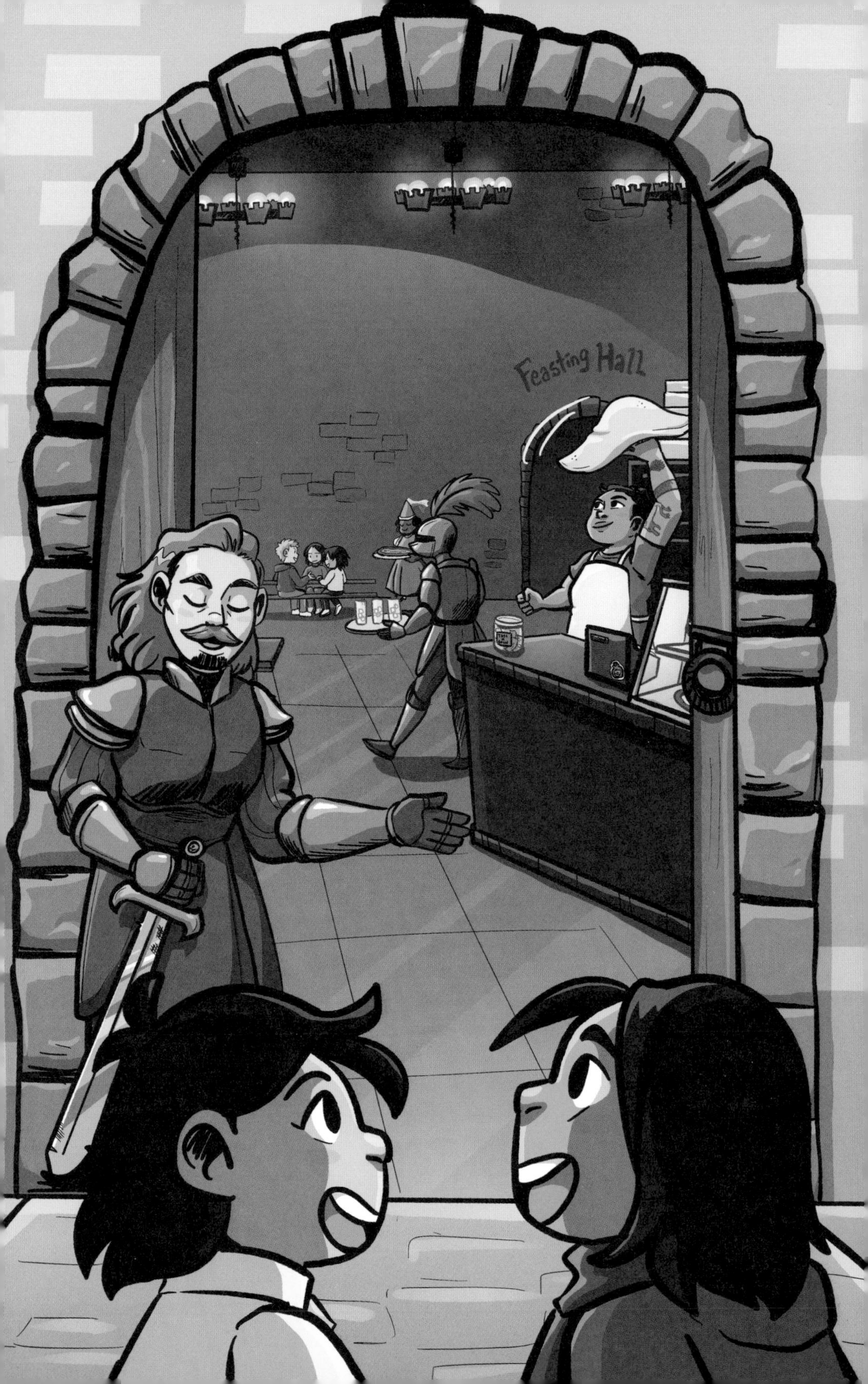
Feasting Hall

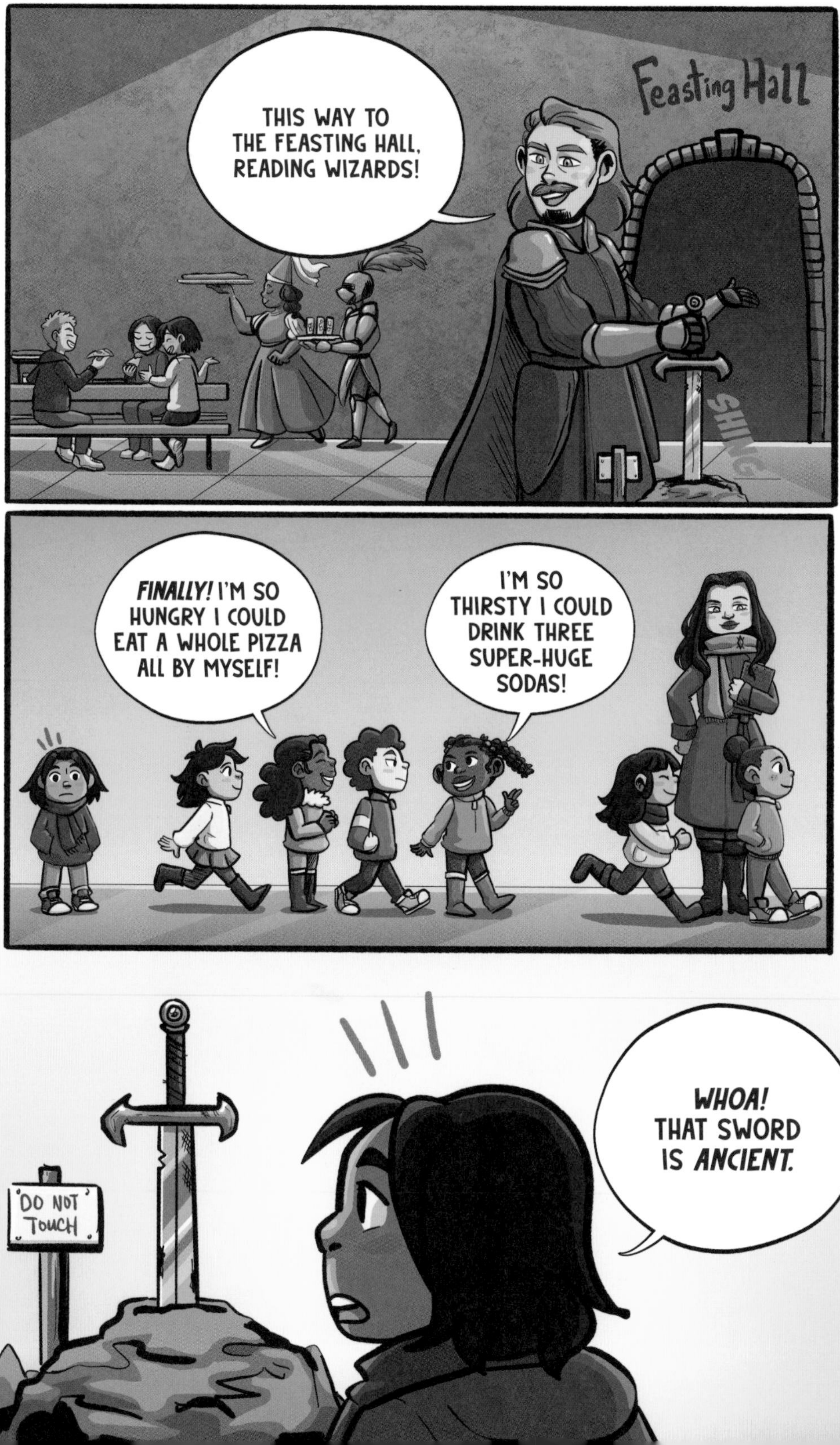
Feasting Hall
THIS WAY TO THE FEASTING HALL, READING WIZARDS!
SHING
FINALLY! I'M SO HUNGRY I COULD EAT A WHOLE PIZZA ALL BY MYSELF!
I'M SO THIRSTY I COULD DRINK THREE SUPER-HUGE SODAS!
DO NOT TOUCH
WHOA! THAT SWORD IS ANCIENT.

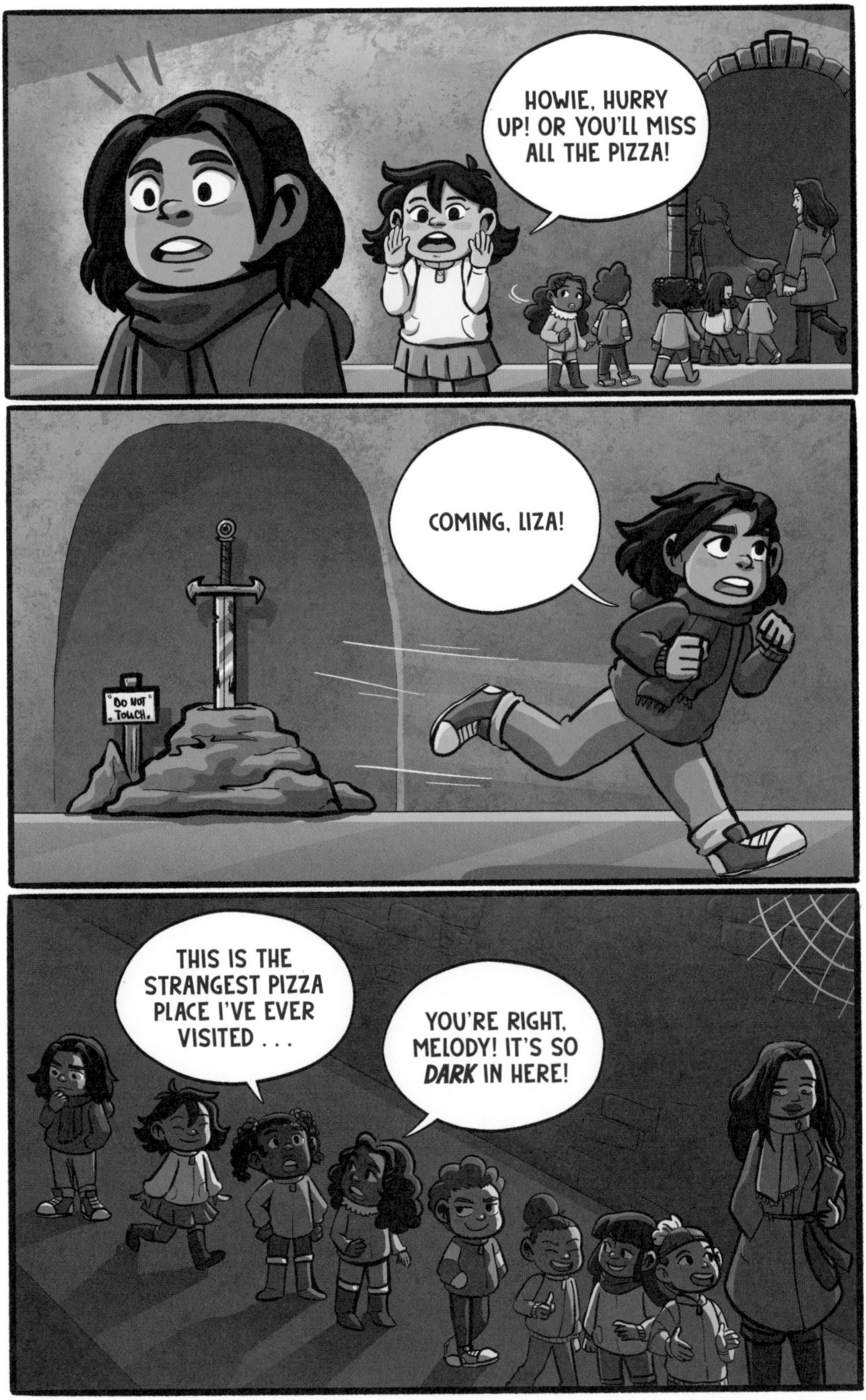
HOWIE, HURRY UP! OR YOU'LL MISS ALL THE PIZZA!
COMING, LIZA!
DO NOT TOUCH.
THIS IS THE STRANGEST PIZZA PLACE I'VE EVER VISITED . . .
YOU'RE RIGHT, MELODY! IT'S SO *DARK* IN HERE!

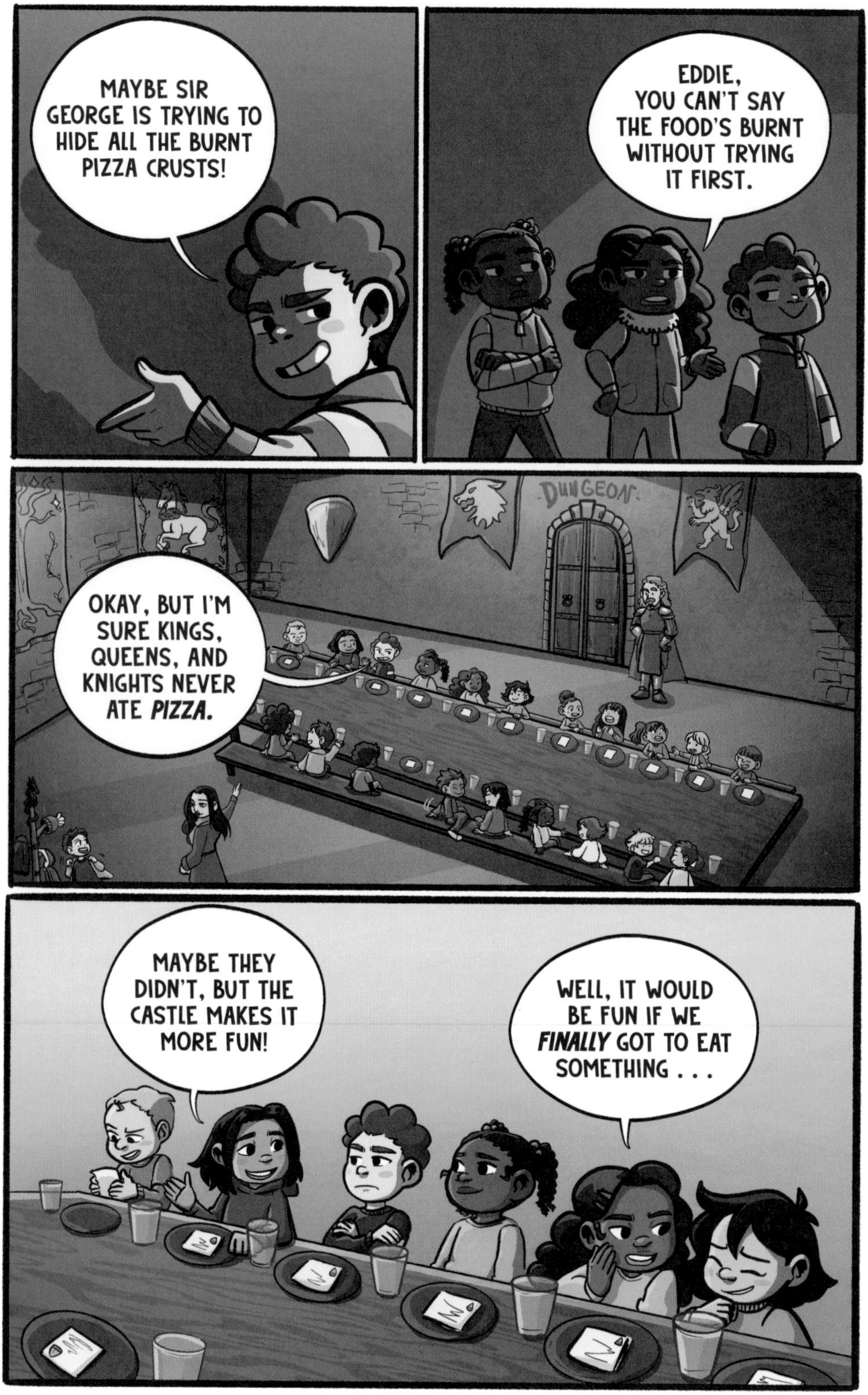
MAYBE SIR GEORGE IS TRYING TO HIDE ALL THE BURNT PIZZA CRUSTS!
EDDIE, YOU CAN'T SAY THE FOOD'S BURNT WITHOUT TRYING IT FIRST.
DUNGEON
OKAY, BUT I'M SURE KINGS, QUEENS, AND KNIGHTS NEVER ATE *PIZZA.*
MAYBE THEY DIDN'T, BUT THE CASTLE MAKES IT MORE FUN!
WELL, IT WOULD BE FUN IF WE *FINALLY* GOT TO EAT SOMETHING . . .

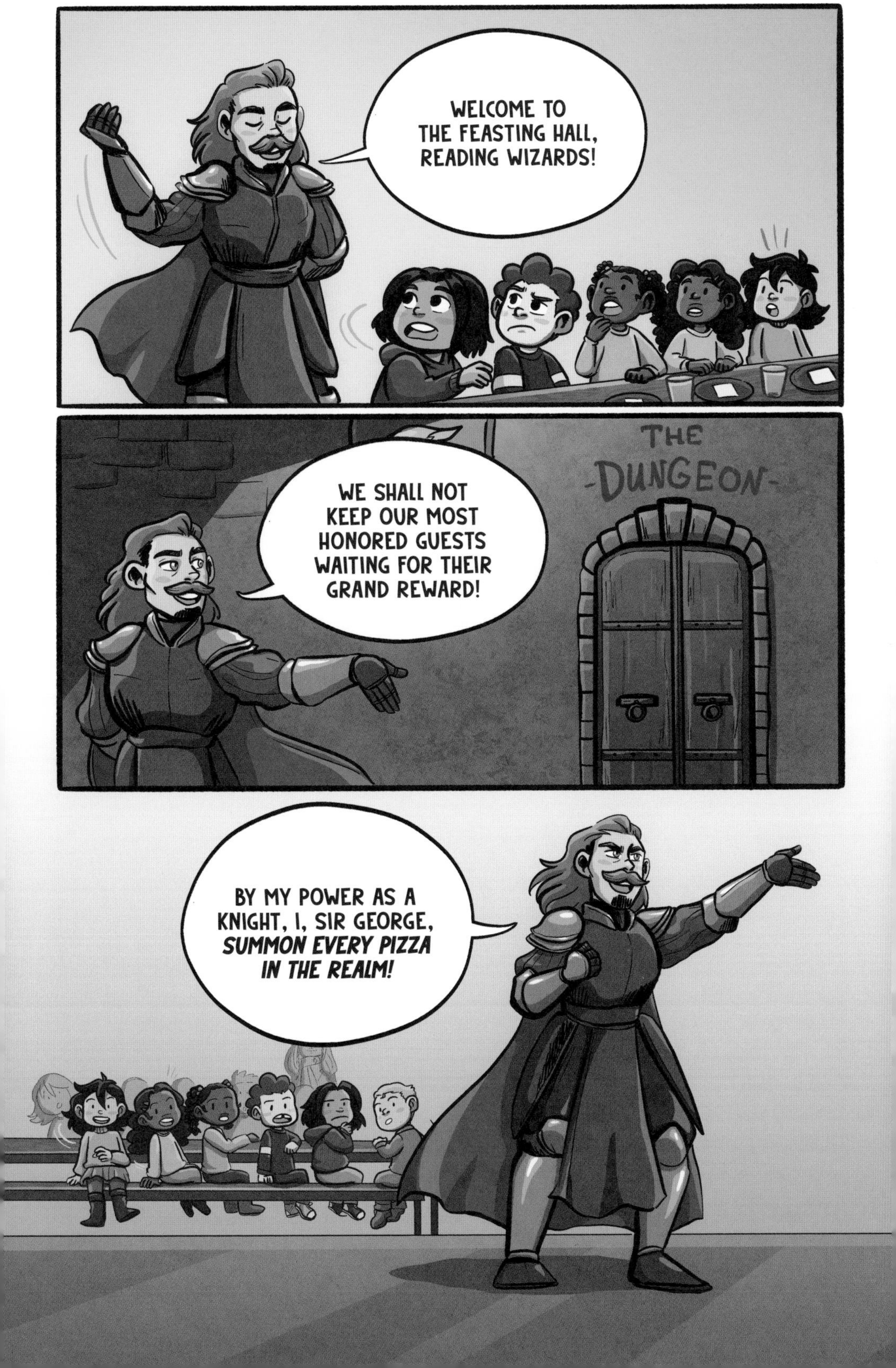
WELCOME TO THE FEASTING HALL, READING WIZARDS!
THE DUNGEON
WE SHALL NOT KEEP OUR MOST HONORED GUESTS WAITING FOR THEIR GRAND REWARD!
BY MY POWER AS A KNIGHT, I, SIR GEORGE, *SUMMON EVERY PIZZA IN THE REALM!*

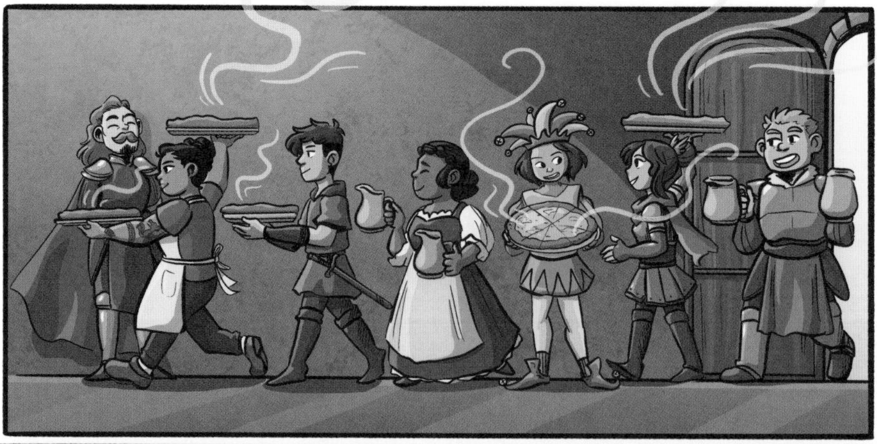

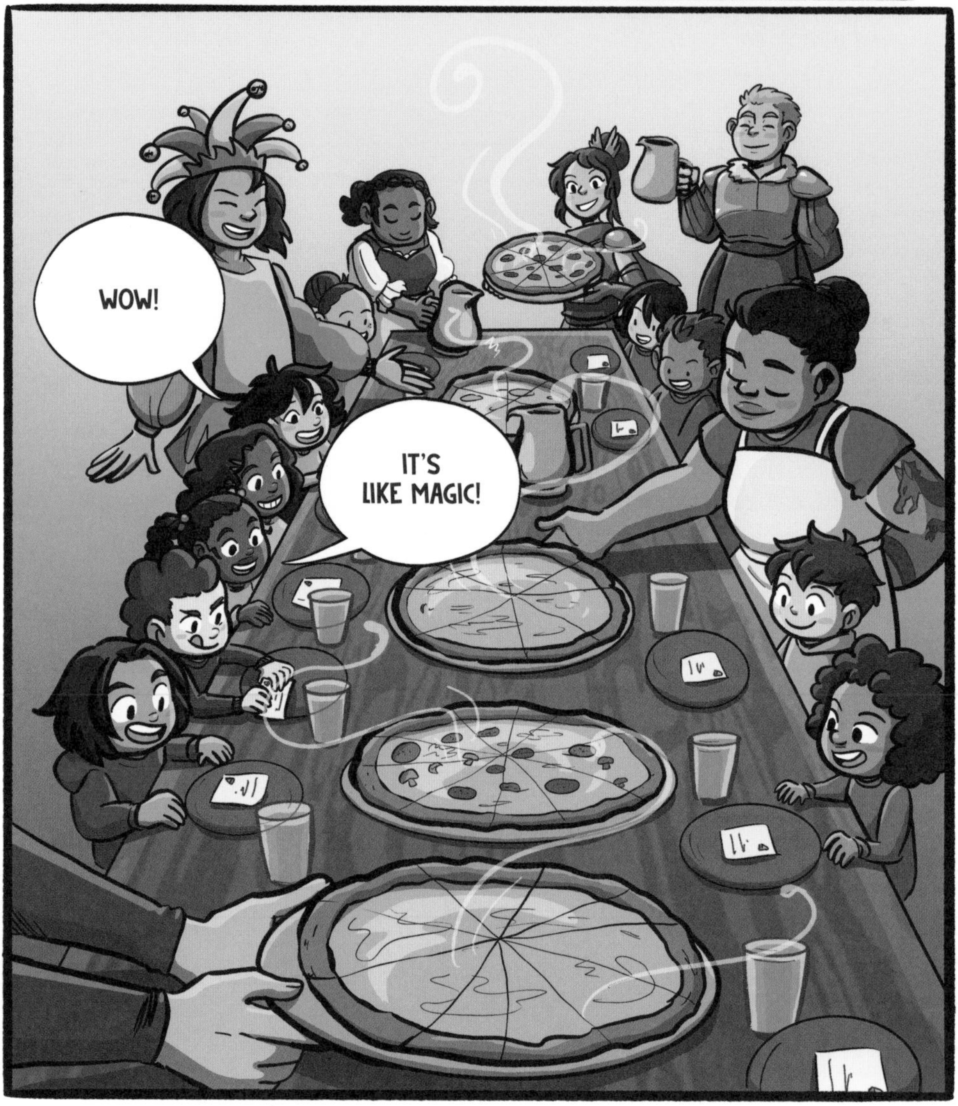
WOW!
IT'S LIKE MAGIC!

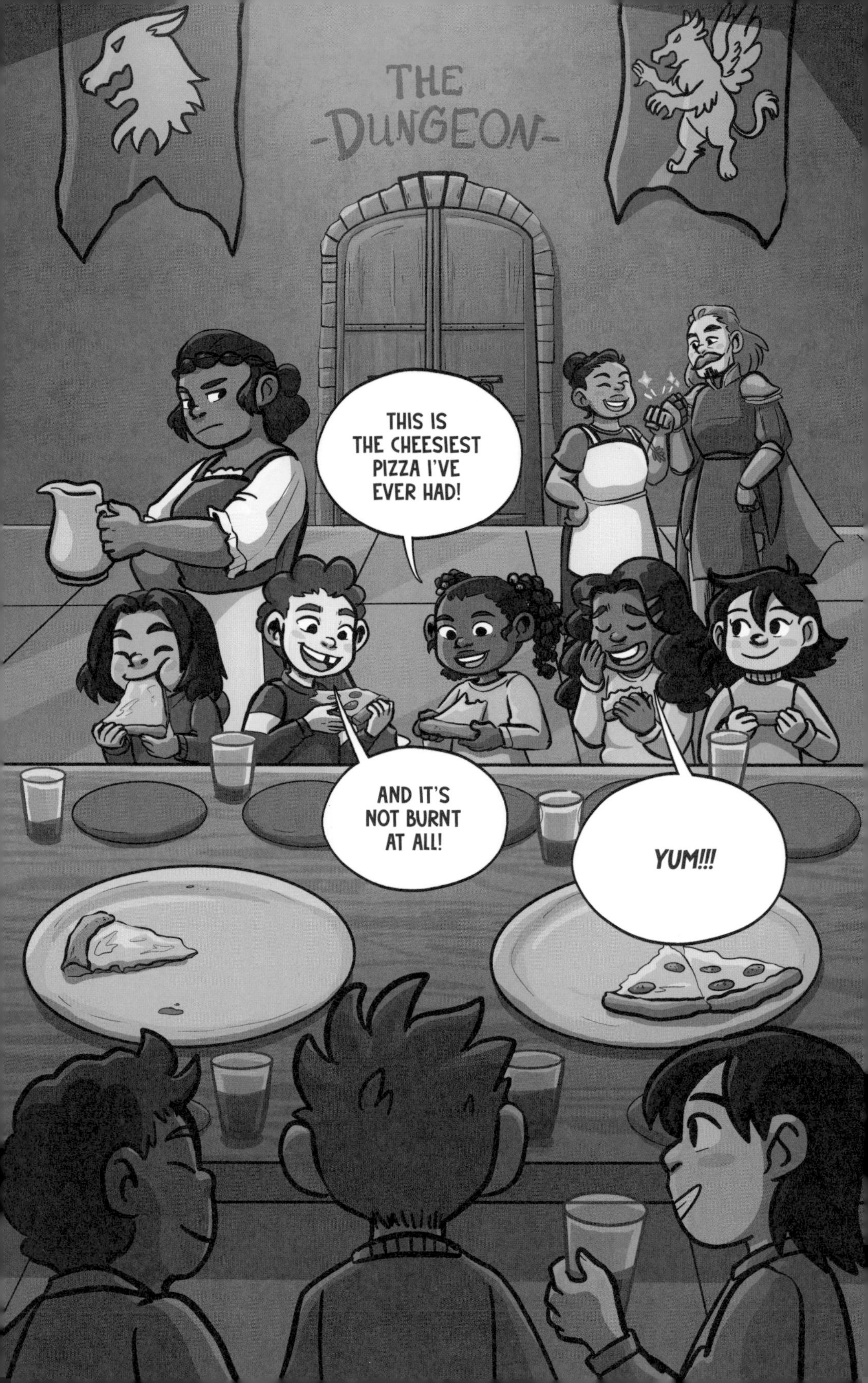
THE DUNGEON
THIS IS THE CHEESIEST PIZZA I'VE EVER HAD!
AND IT'S NOT BURNT AT ALL!
YUM!!!

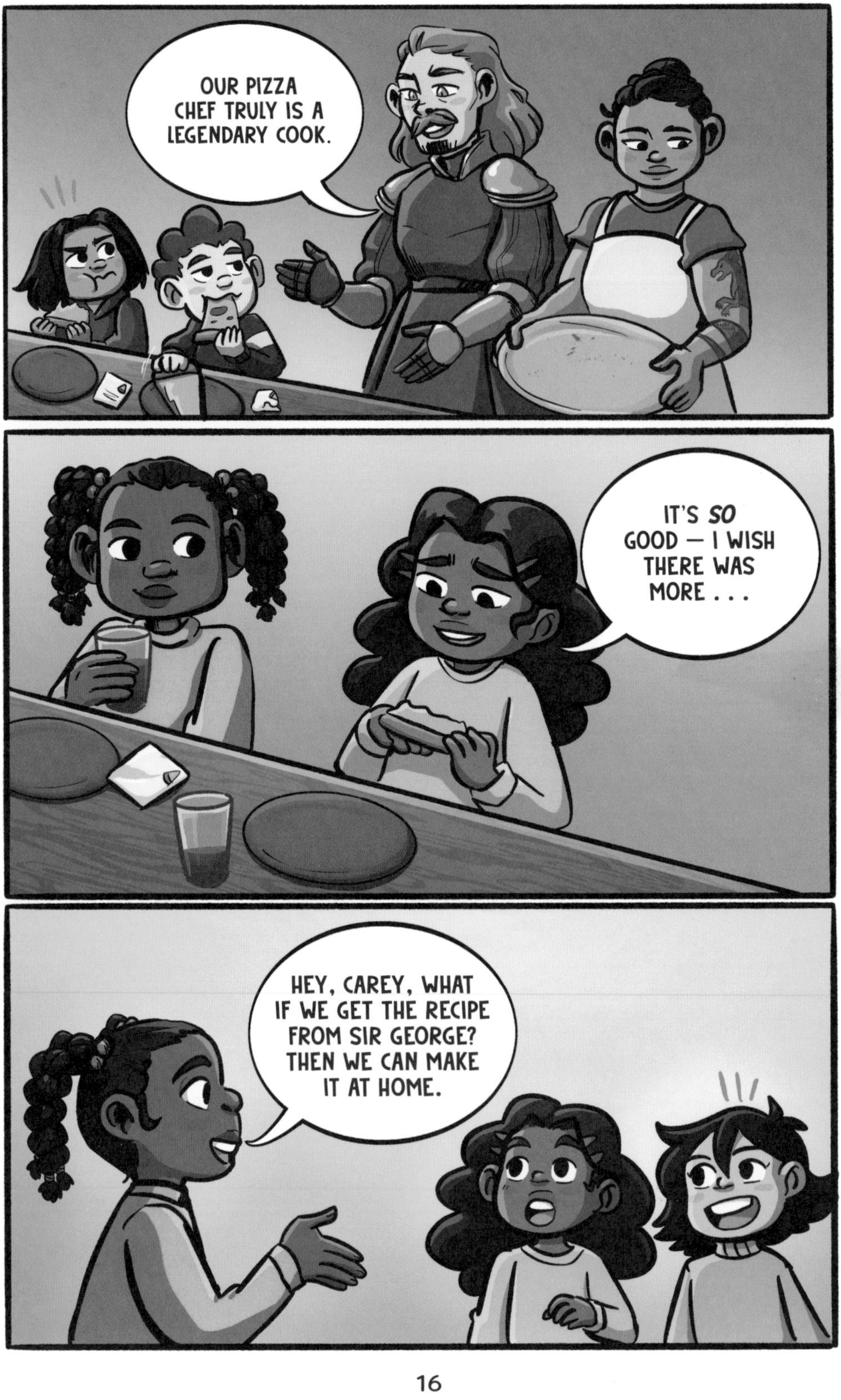
OUR PIZZA CHEF TRULY IS A LEGENDARY COOK.
IT'S *SO* GOOD — I WISH THERE WAS MORE . . .
HEY, CAREY, WHAT IF WE GET THE RECIPE FROM SIR GEORGE? THEN WE CAN MAKE IT AT HOME.

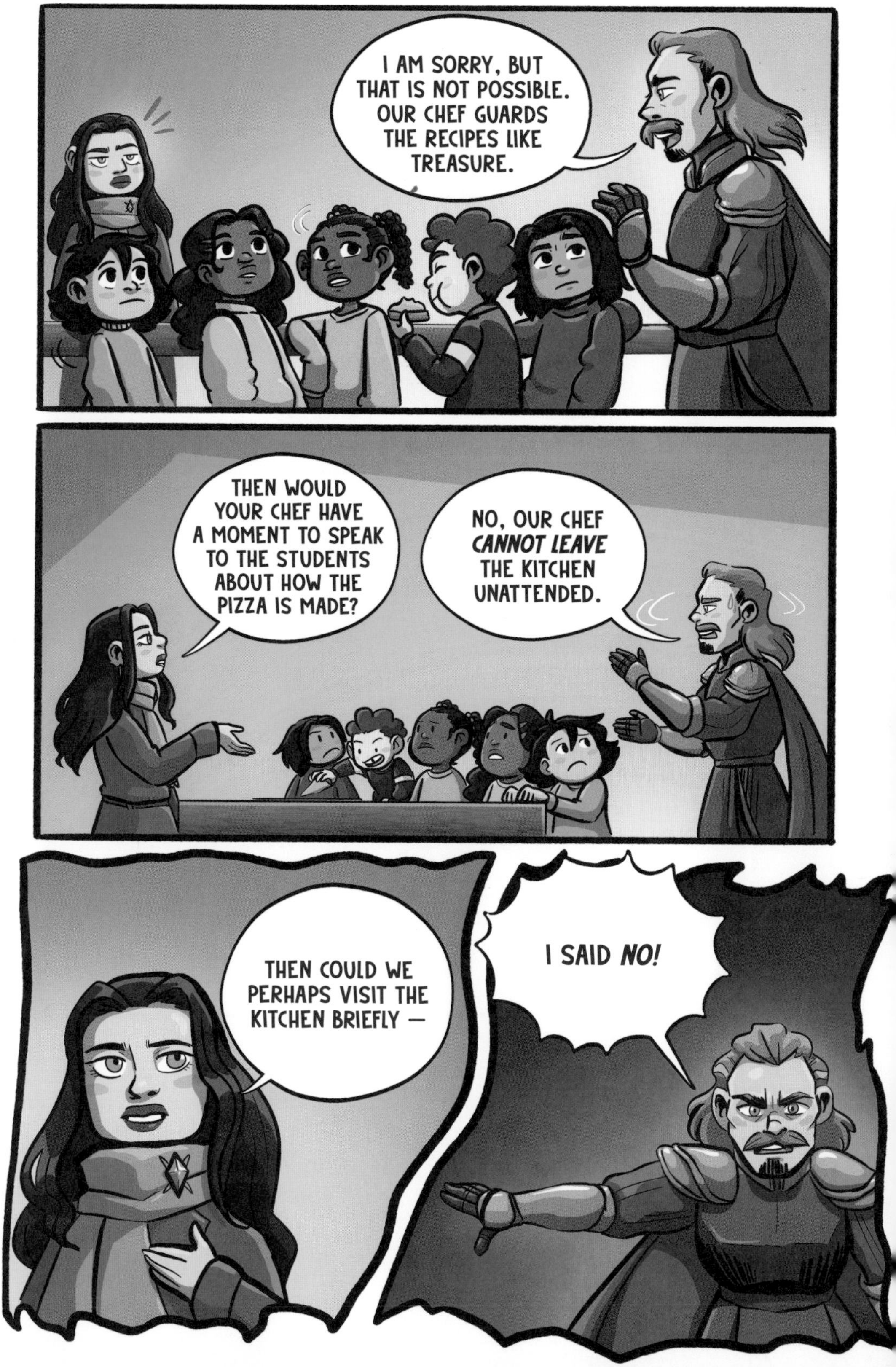
I AM SORRY, BUT THAT IS NOT POSSIBLE. OUR CHEF GUARDS THE RECIPES LIKE TREASURE.
THEN WOULD YOUR CHEF HAVE A MOMENT TO SPEAK TO THE STUDENTS ABOUT HOW THE PIZZA IS MADE?
NO, OUR CHEF *CANNOT LEAVE* THE KITCHEN UNATTENDED.
THEN COULD WE PERHAPS VISIT THE KITCHEN BRIEFLY —
I SAID *NO!*

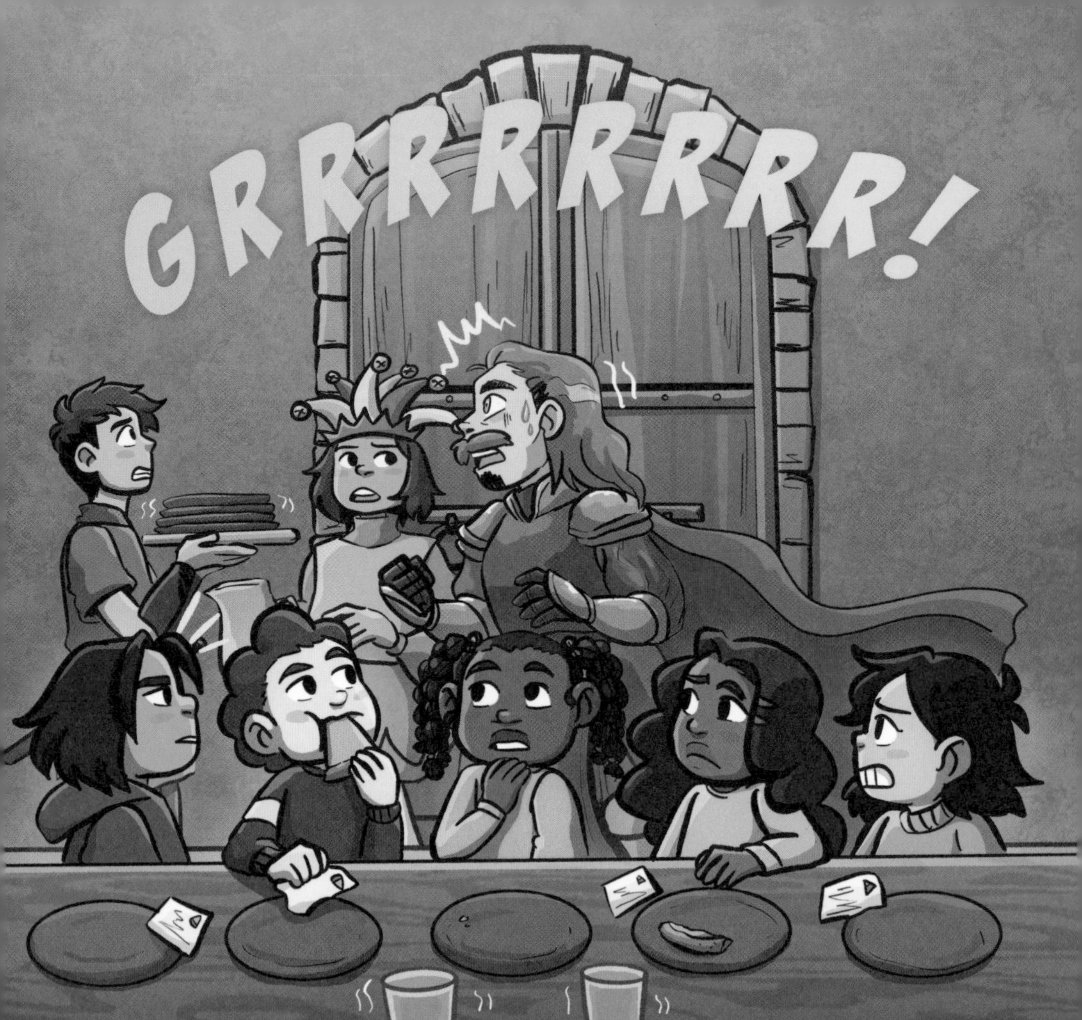
GRRRRRRRRR!

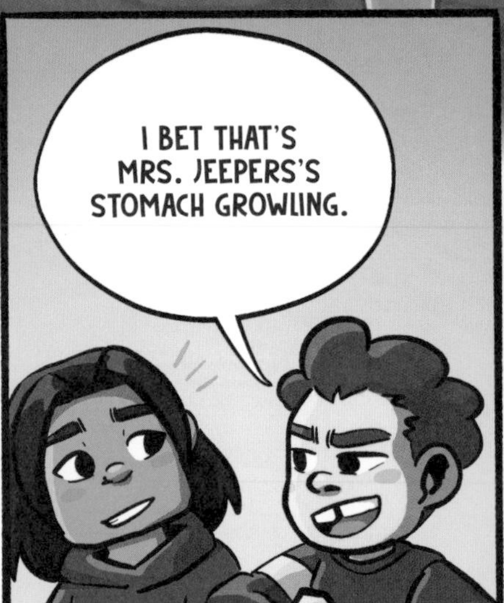
I BET THAT'S MRS. JEEPERS'S STOMACH GROWLING.

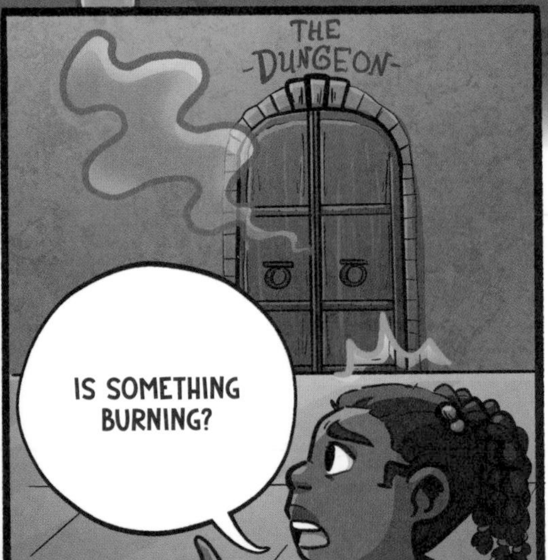
THE -DUNGEON-
IS SOMETHING BURNING?

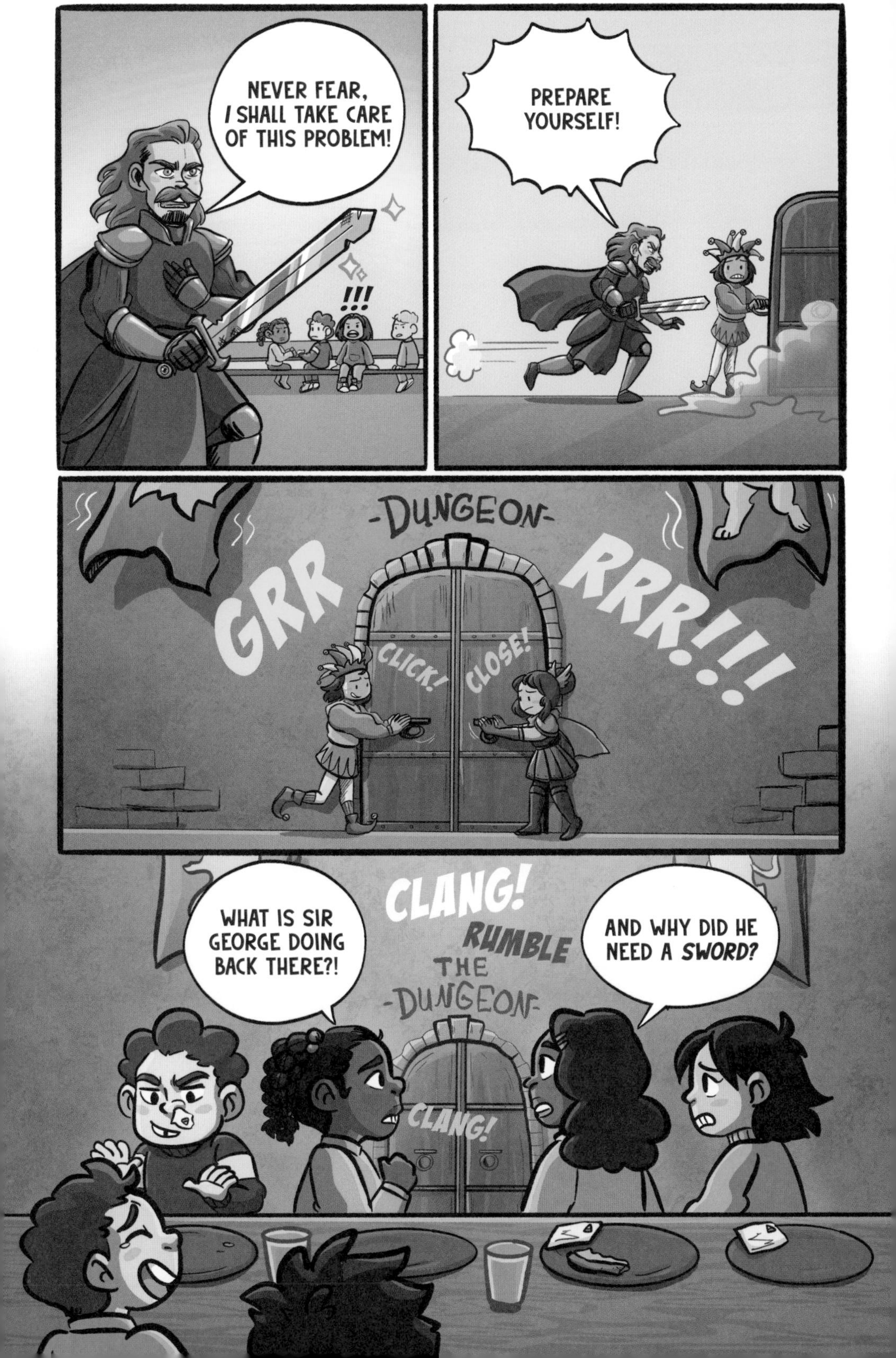
NEVER FEAR, I SHALL TAKE CARE OF THIS PROBLEM!
!!!
PREPARE YOURSELF!
-DUNGEON-
GRR
RRR!!!!
CLICK!
CLOSE!
CLANG!
RUMBLE
WHAT IS SIR GEORGE DOING BACK THERE?!
AND WHY DID HE NEED A *SWORD*?
THE -DUNGEON-
CLANG!

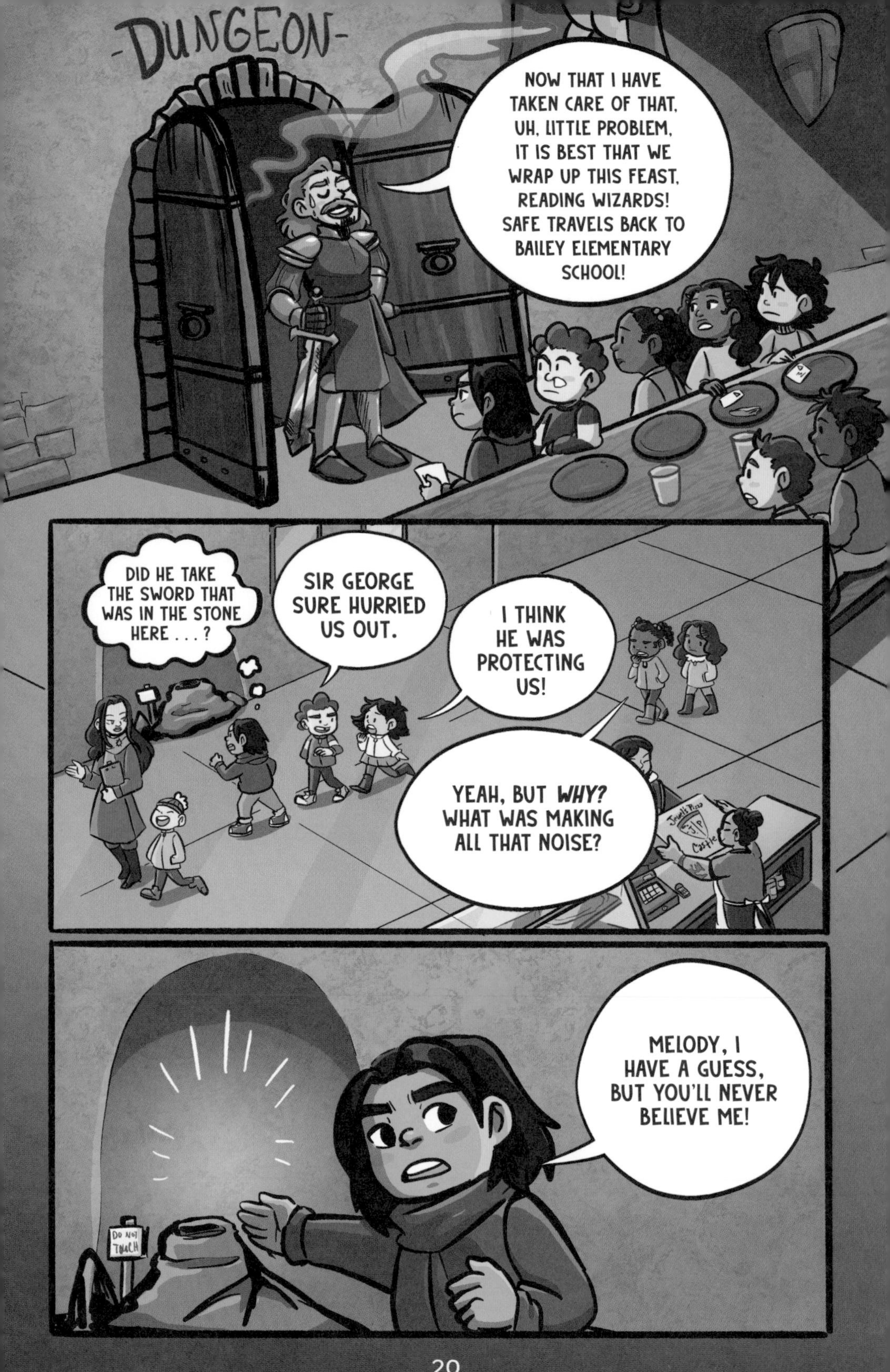
-DUNGEON-
NOW THAT I HAVE TAKEN CARE OF THAT, UH, LITTLE PROBLEM, IT IS BEST THAT WE WRAP UP THIS FEAST, READING WIZARDS! SAFE TRAVELS BACK TO BAILEY ELEMENTARY SCHOOL!
DID HE TAKE THE SWORD THAT WAS IN THE STONE HERE . . . ?
SIR GEORGE SURE HURRIED US OUT.
I THINK HE WAS PROTECTING US!
YEAH, BUT *WHY?* WHAT WAS MAKING ALL THAT NOISE?
MELODY, I HAVE A GUESS, BUT YOU'LL NEVER BELIEVE ME!
DO NOT TOUCH

CHAPTER 2 SAINT GEORGE AND THE DRAGON

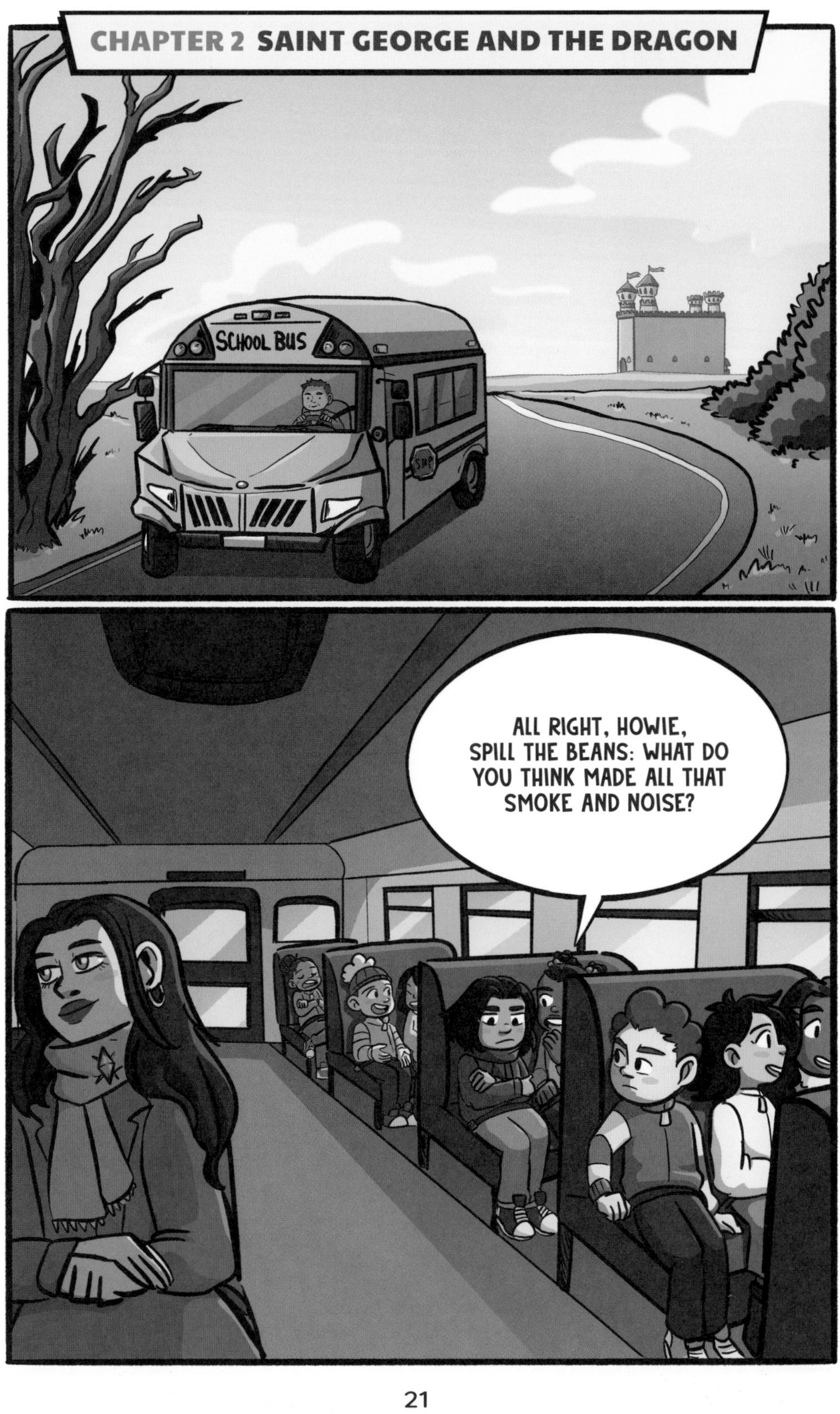
SCHOOL BUS
ALL RIGHT, HOWIE, SPILL THE BEANS: WHAT DO YOU THINK MADE ALL THAT SMOKE AND NOISE?

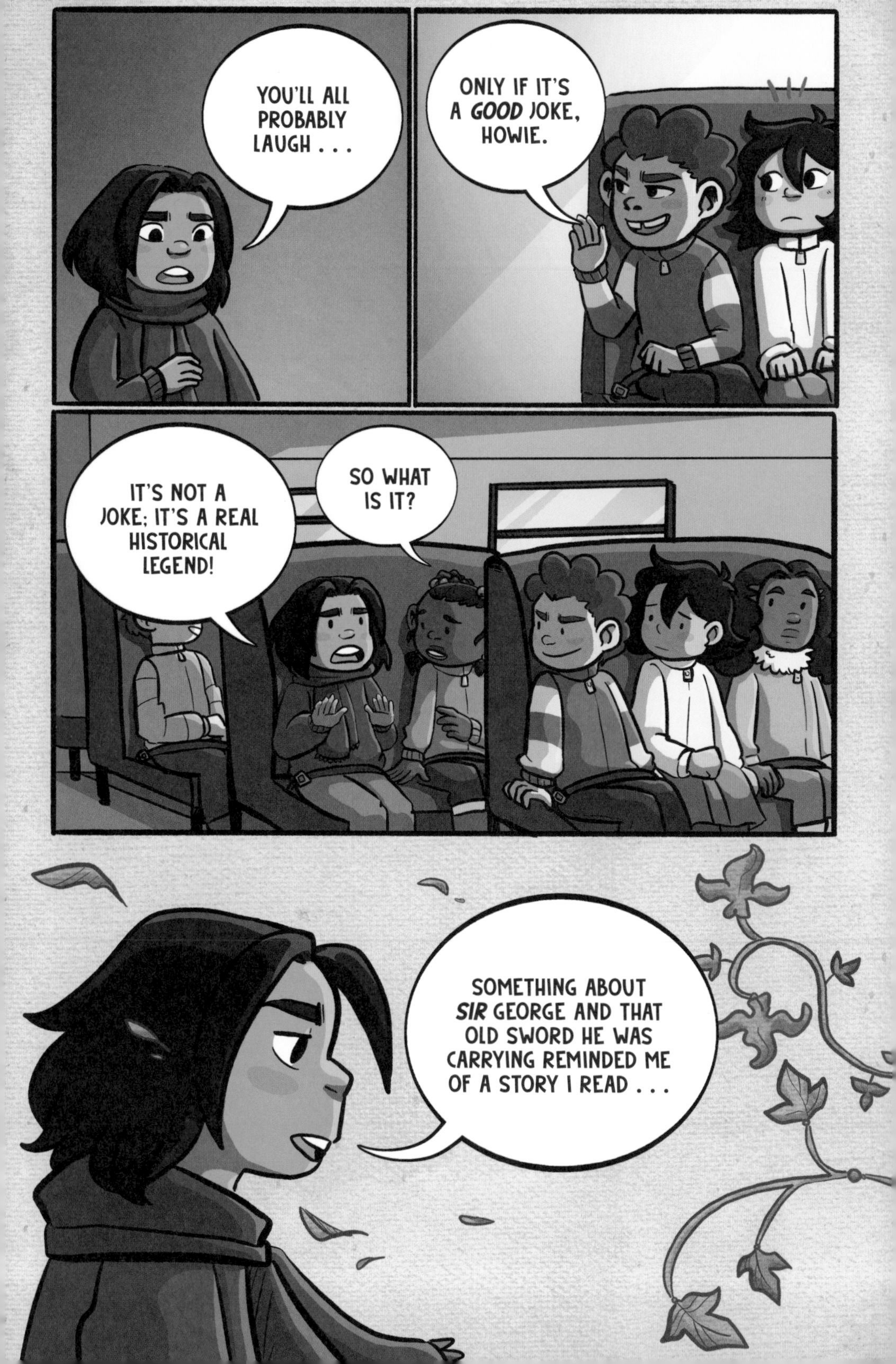
YOU'LL ALL PROBABLY LAUGH . . .
ONLY IF IT'S A *GOOD* JOKE, HOWIE.
IT'S NOT A JOKE; IT'S A REAL HISTORICAL LEGEND!
SO WHAT IS IT?
SOMETHING ABOUT *SIR* GEORGE AND THAT OLD SWORD HE WAS CARRYING REMINDED ME OF A STORY I READ . . .

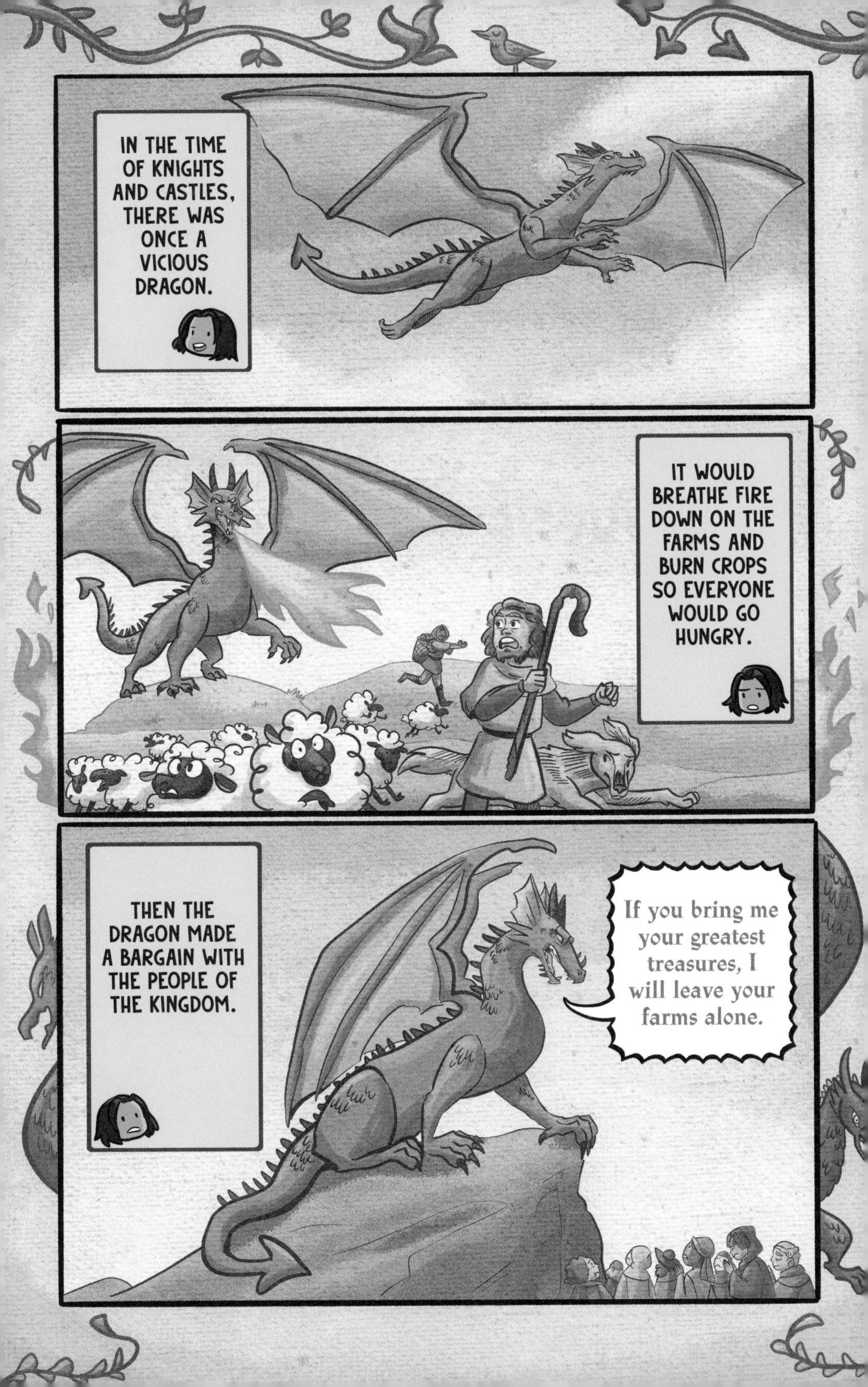
IN THE TIME OF KNIGHTS AND CASTLES, THERE WAS ONCE A VICIOUS DRAGON.
IT WOULD BREATHE FIRE DOWN ON THE FARMS AND BURN CROPS SO EVERYONE WOULD GO HUNGRY.
THEN THE DRAGON MADE A BARGAIN WITH THE PEOPLE OF THE KINGDOM.
If you bring me your greatest treasures, I will leave your farms alone.

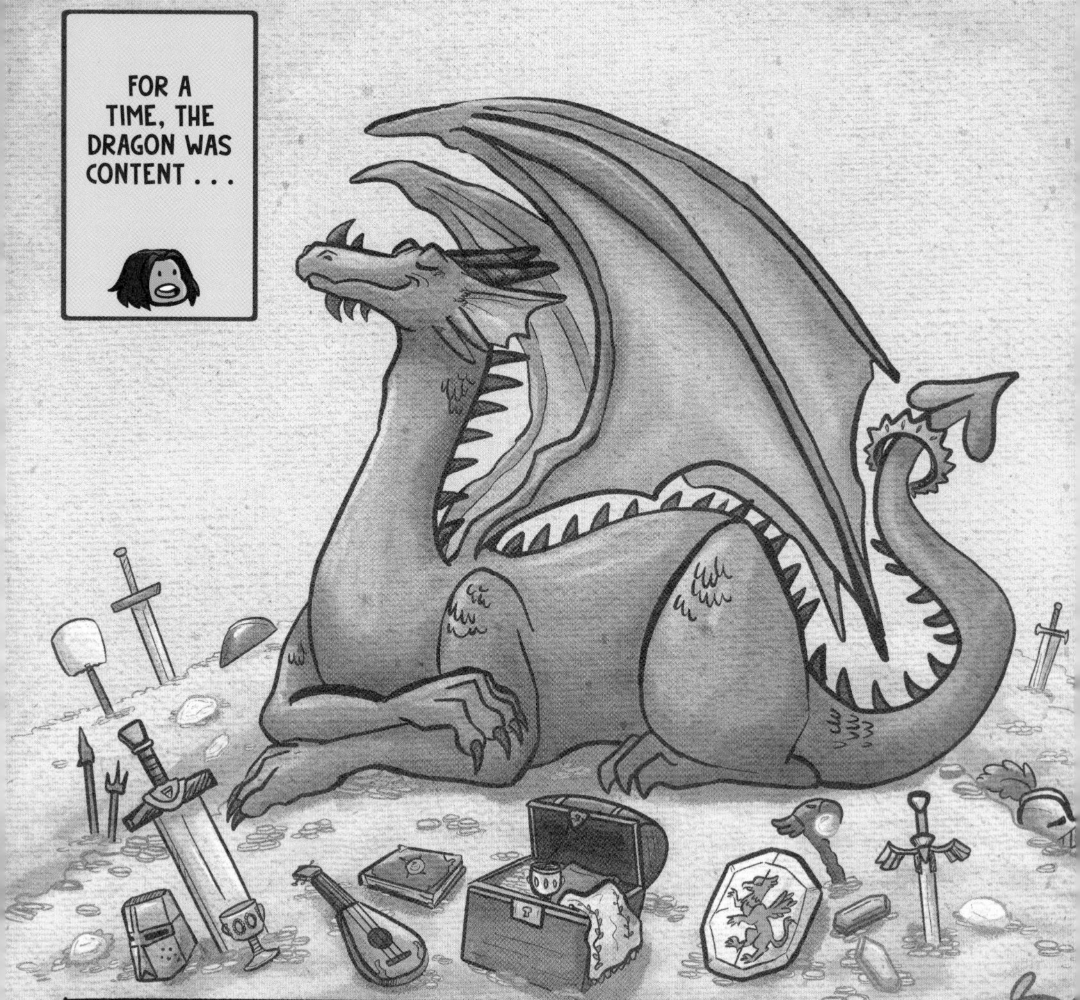
FOR A TIME, THE DRAGON WAS CONTENT . . .

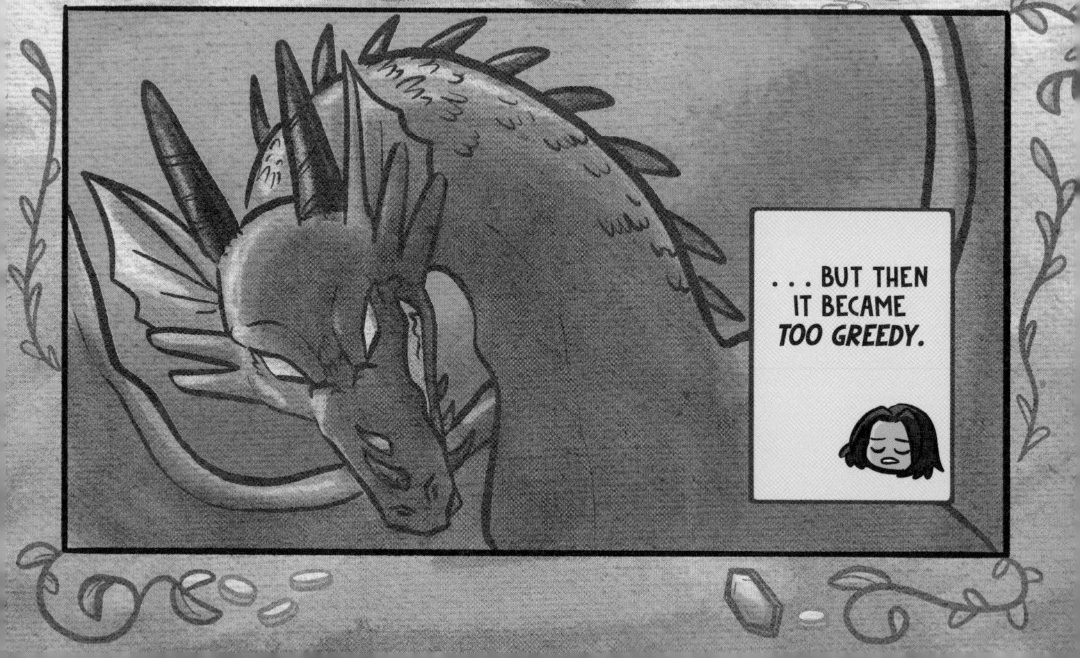
. . . BUT THEN IT BECAME *TOO GREEDY.*

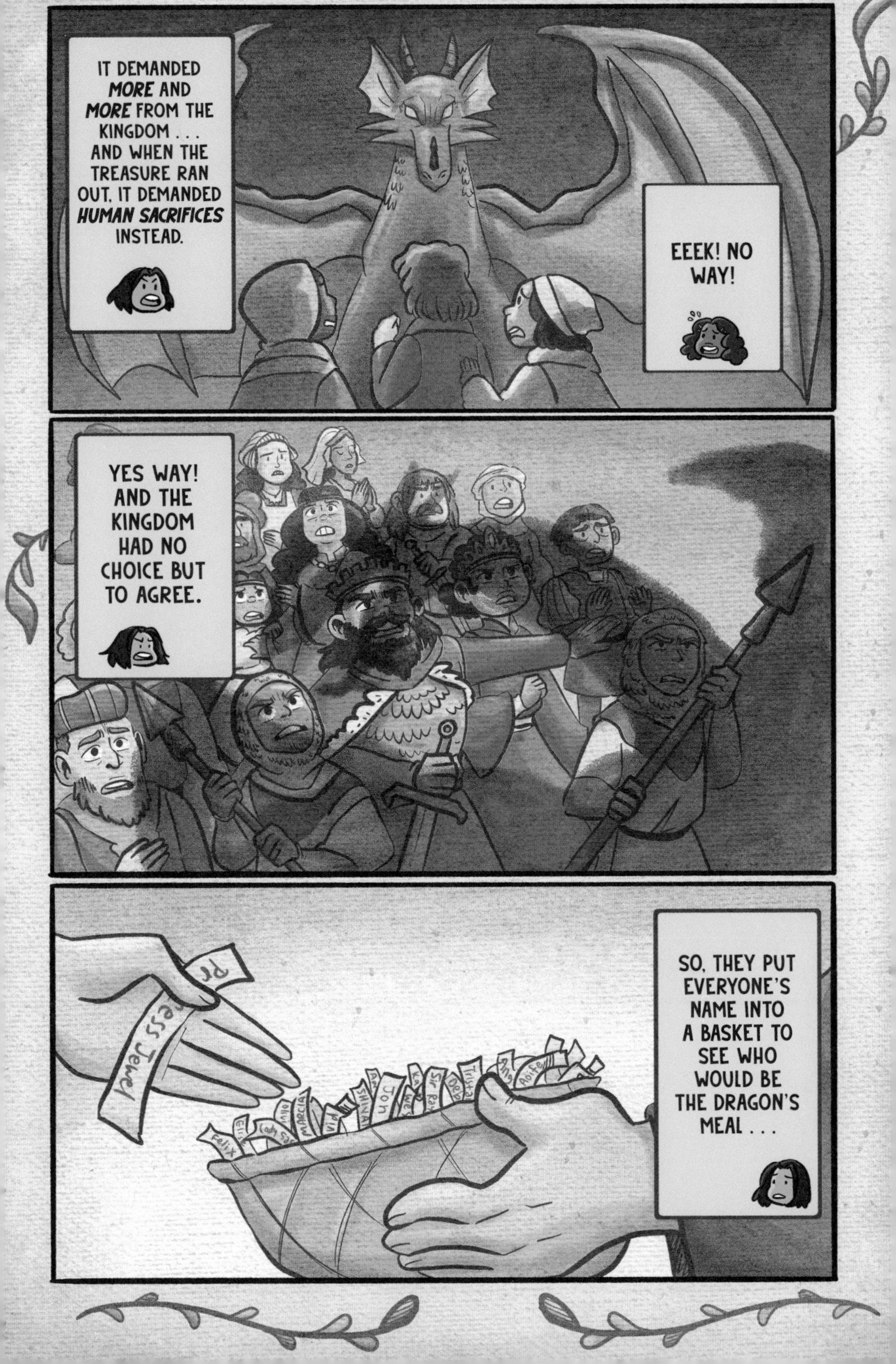
IT DEMANDED *MORE* AND *MORE* FROM THE KINGDOM . . . AND WHEN THE TREASURE RAN OUT, IT DEMANDED *HUMAN SACRIFICES* INSTEAD.
EEEK! NO WAY!
YES WAY! AND THE KINGDOM HAD NO CHOICE BUT TO AGREE.
SO, THEY PUT EVERYONE'S NAME INTO A BASKET TO SEE WHO WOULD BE THE DRAGON'S MEAL . . .

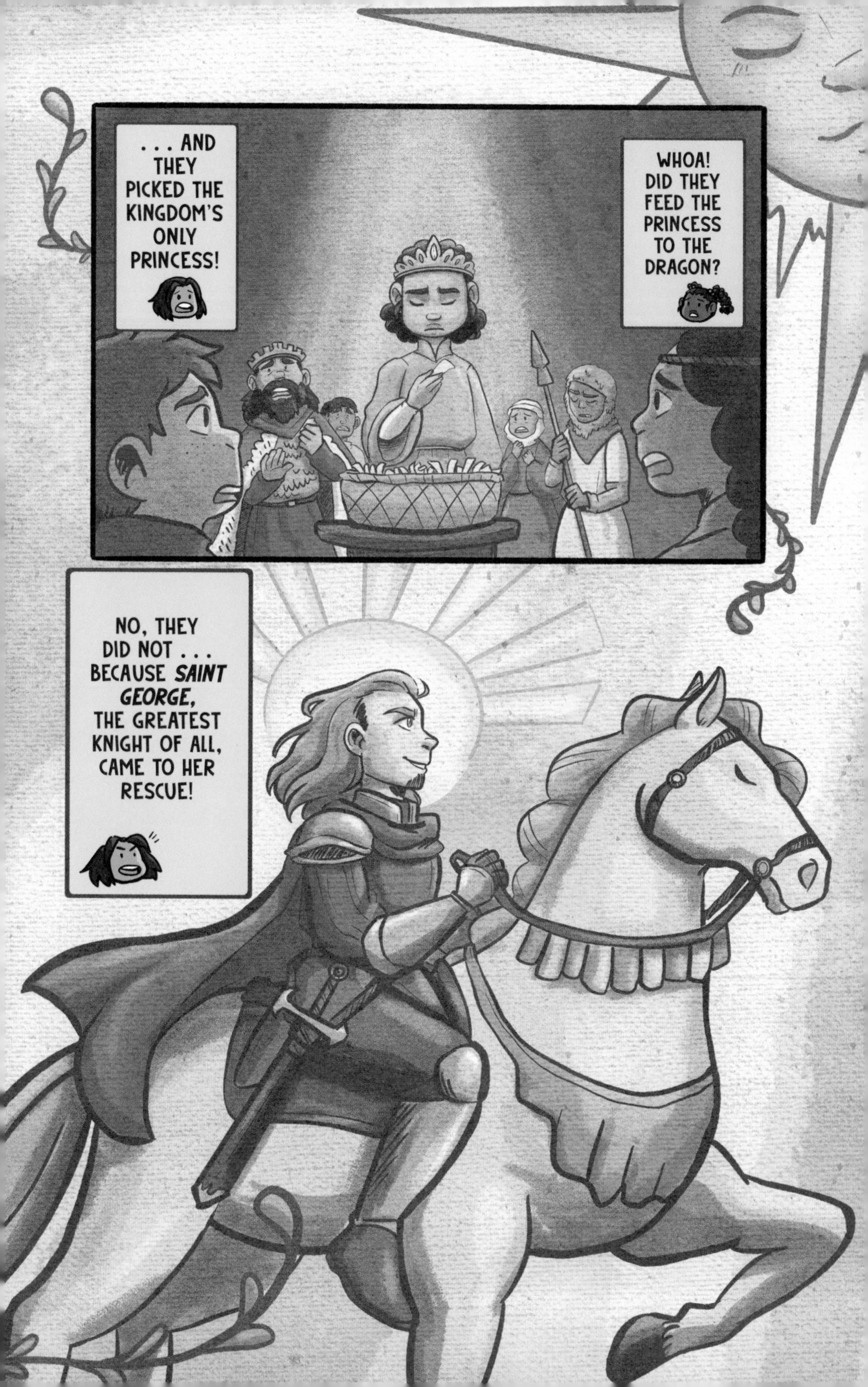
. . . AND THEY PICKED THE KINGDOM'S ONLY PRINCESS!
WHOA! DID THEY FEED THE PRINCESS TO THE DRAGON?
NO, THEY DID NOT . . . BECAUSE *SAINT GEORGE*, THE GREATEST KNIGHT OF ALL, CAME TO HER RESCUE!

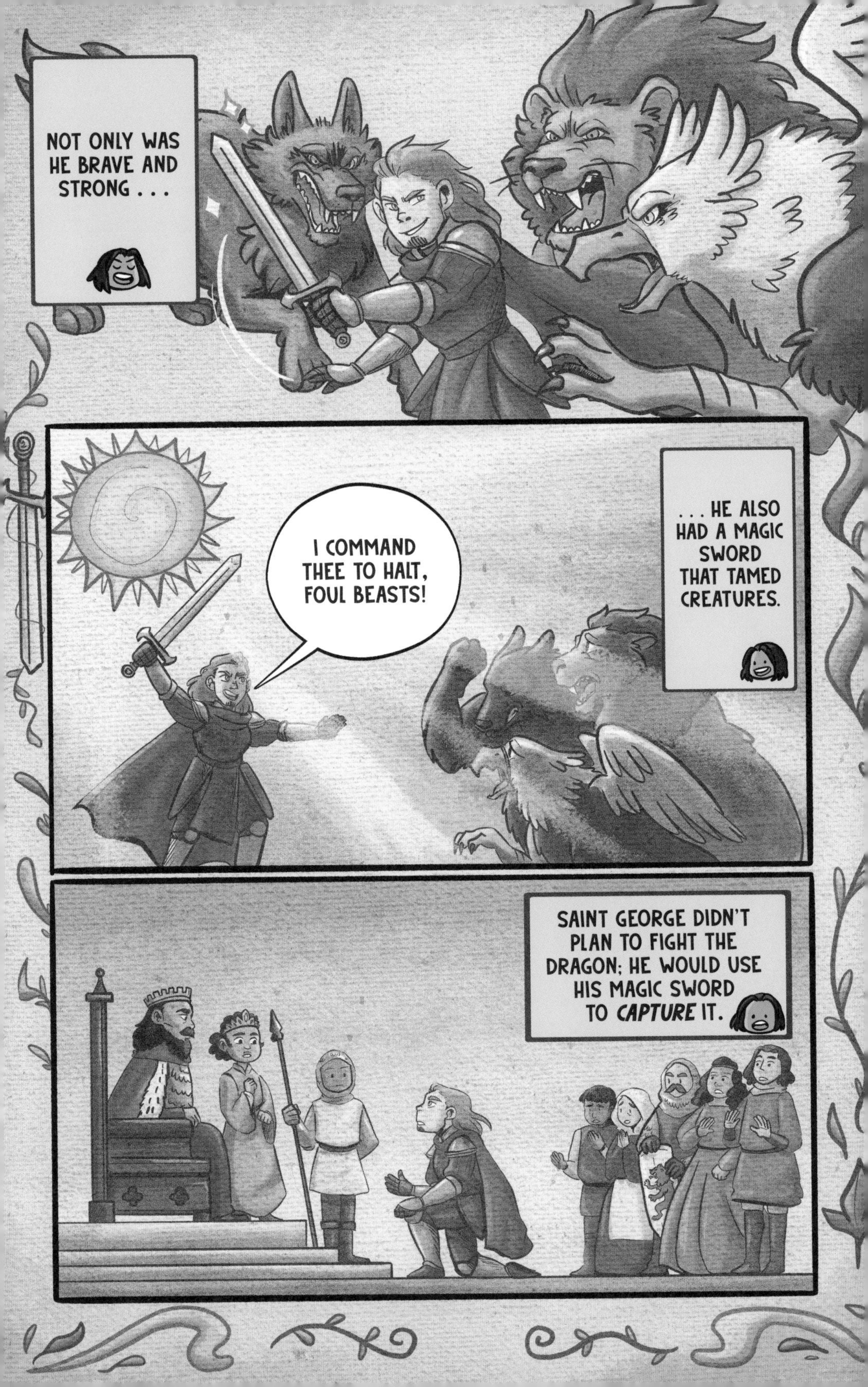
NOT ONLY WAS HE BRAVE AND STRONG . . .
I COMMAND THEE TO HALT, FOUL BEASTS!
. . . HE ALSO HAD A MAGIC SWORD THAT TAMED CREATURES.
SAINT GEORGE DIDN'T PLAN TO FIGHT THE DRAGON; HE WOULD USE HIS MAGIC SWORD TO *CAPTURE* IT.

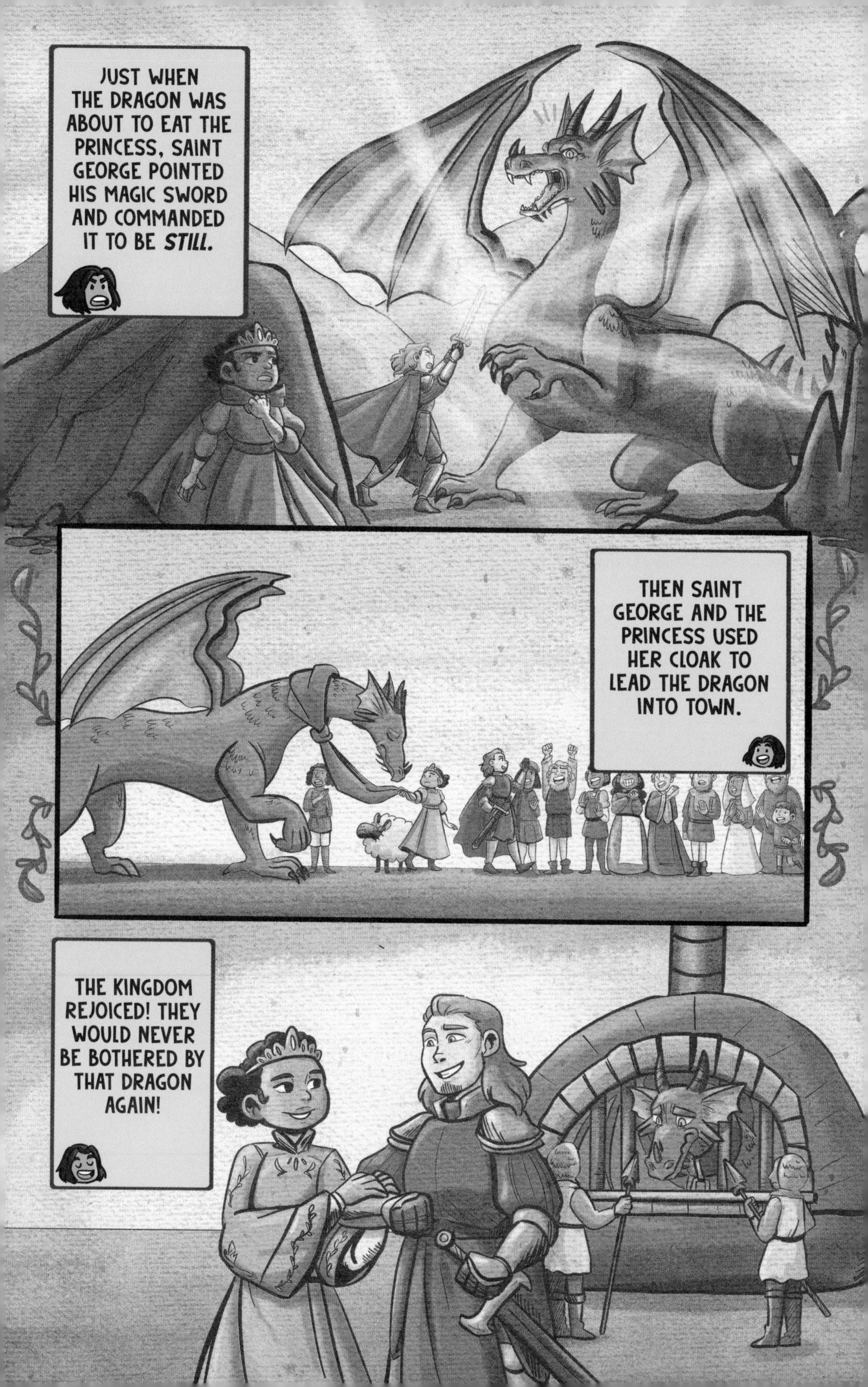
JUST WHEN THE DRAGON WAS ABOUT TO EAT THE PRINCESS, SAINT GEORGE POINTED HIS MAGIC SWORD AND COMMANDED IT TO BE *STILL.*
THEN SAINT GEORGE AND THE PRINCESS USED HER CLOAK TO LEAD THE DRAGON INTO TOWN.
THE KINGDOM REJOICED! THEY WOULD NEVER BE BOTHERED BY THAT DRAGON AGAIN!

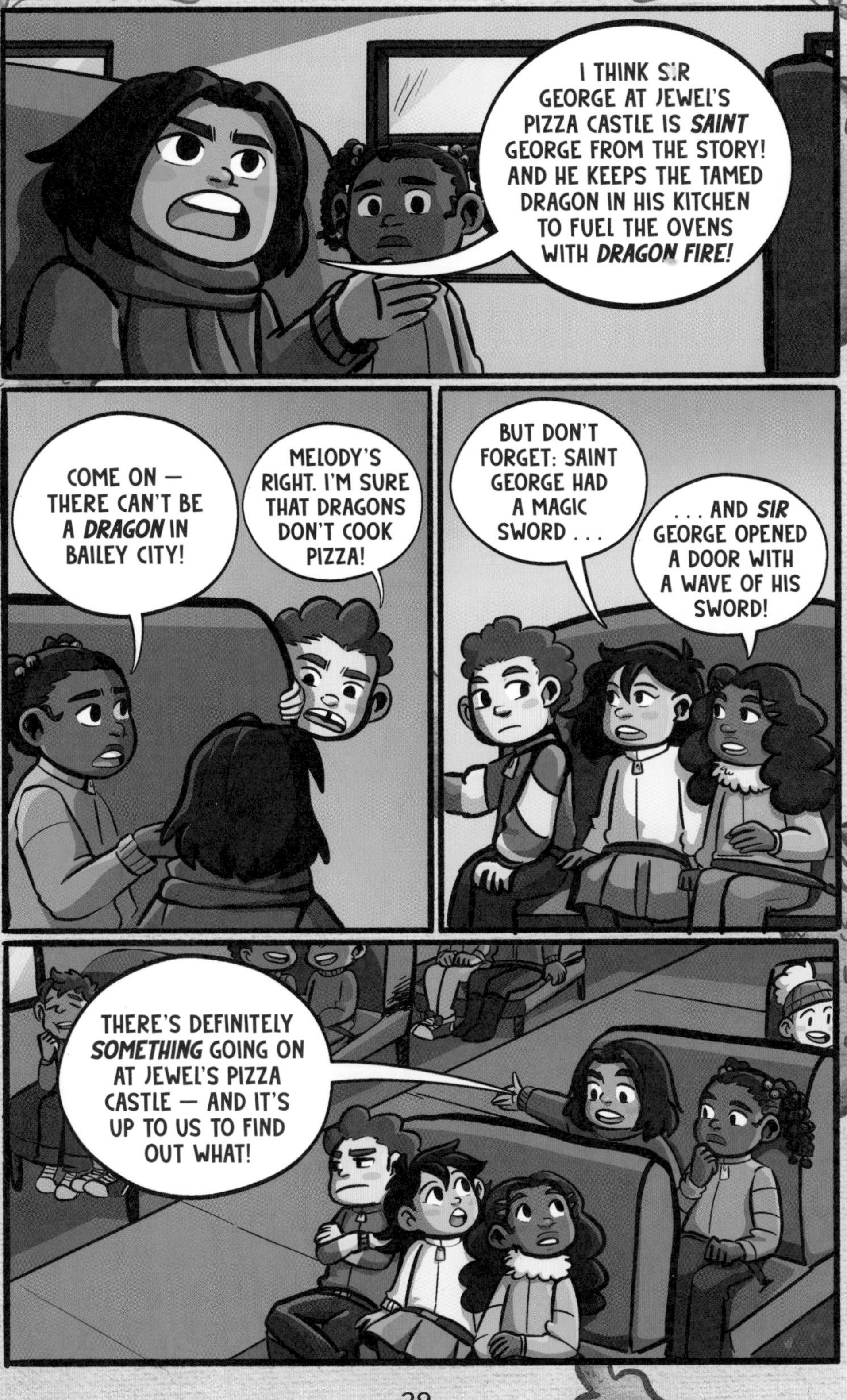
I THINK SIR GEORGE AT JEWEL'S PIZZA CASTLE IS *SAINT* GEORGE FROM THE STORY! AND HE KEEPS THE TAMED DRAGON IN HIS KITCHEN TO FUEL THE OVENS WITH *DRAGON FIRE!*
COME ON — THERE CAN'T BE A *DRAGON* IN BAILEY CITY!
MELODY'S RIGHT. I'M SURE THAT DRAGONS DON'T COOK PIZZA!
BUT DON'T FORGET: SAINT GEORGE HAD A MAGIC SWORD . . .
. . . AND *SIR* GEORGE OPENED A DOOR WITH A WAVE OF HIS SWORD!
THERE'S DEFINITELY *SOMETHING* GOING ON AT JEWEL'S PIZZA CASTLE — AND IT'S UP TO US TO FIND OUT WHAT!

CHAPTER 3 THE RIDDLE

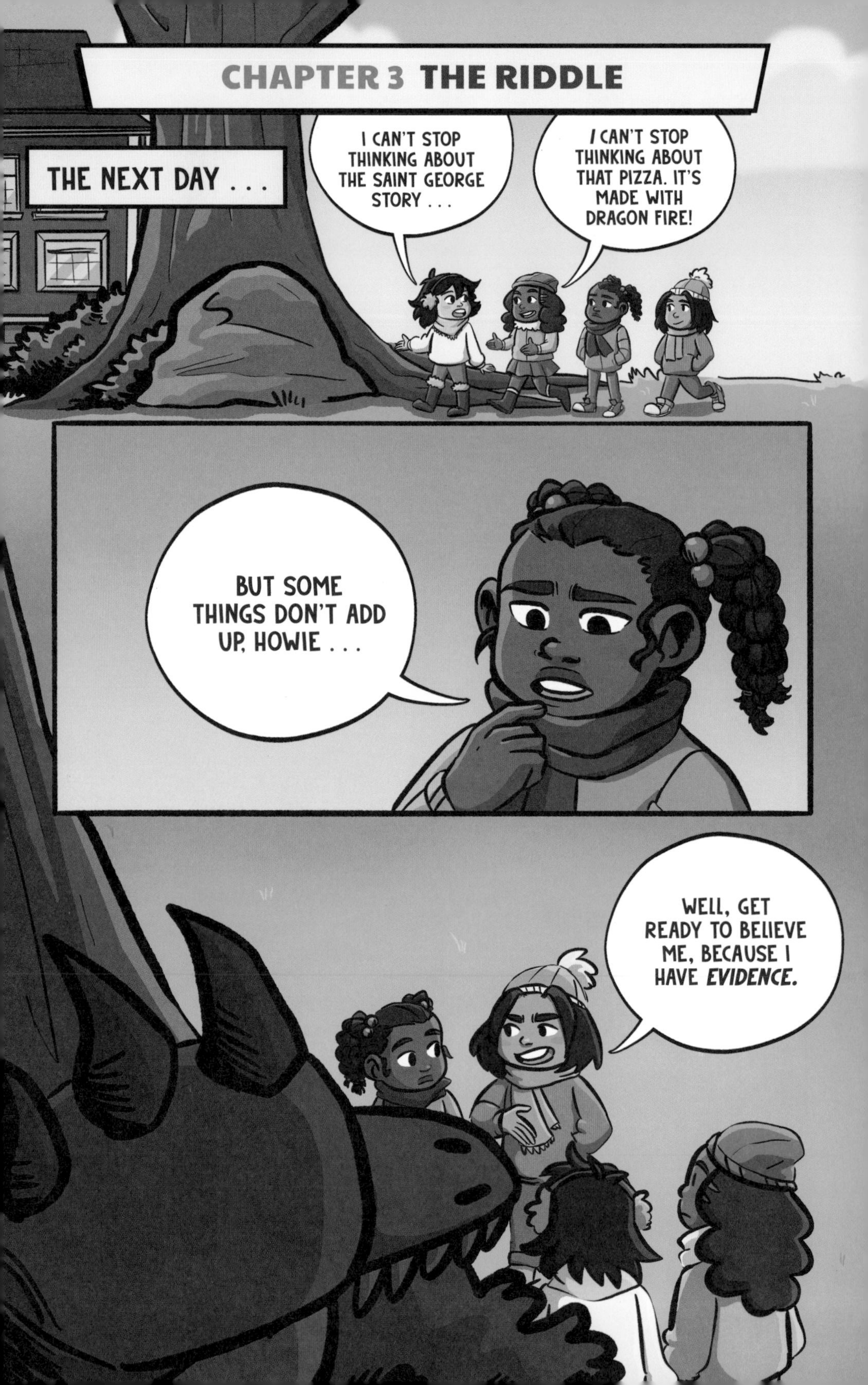
THE NEXT DAY . . .
I CAN'T STOP THINKING ABOUT THE SAINT GEORGE STORY . . .
I CAN'T STOP THINKING ABOUT THAT PIZZA. IT'S MADE WITH DRAGON FIRE!
BUT SOME THINGS DON'T ADD UP, HOWIE . . .
WELL, GET READY TO BELIEVE ME, BECAUSE I HAVE *EVIDENCE.*

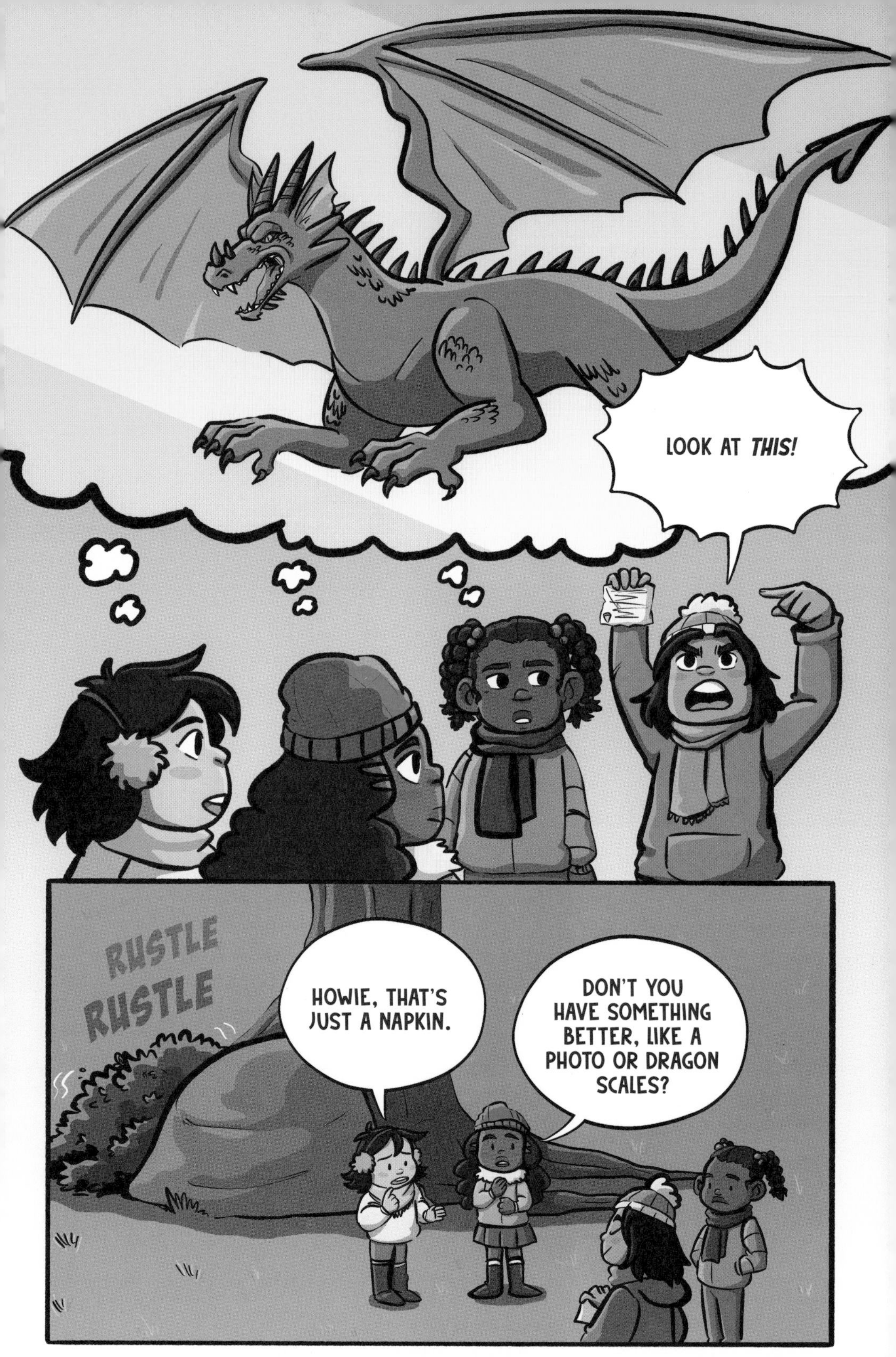
LOOK AT *THIS!*
RUSTLE RUSTLE
HOWIE, THAT'S JUST A NAPKIN.
DON'T YOU HAVE SOMETHING BETTER, LIKE A PHOTO OR DRAGON SCALES?

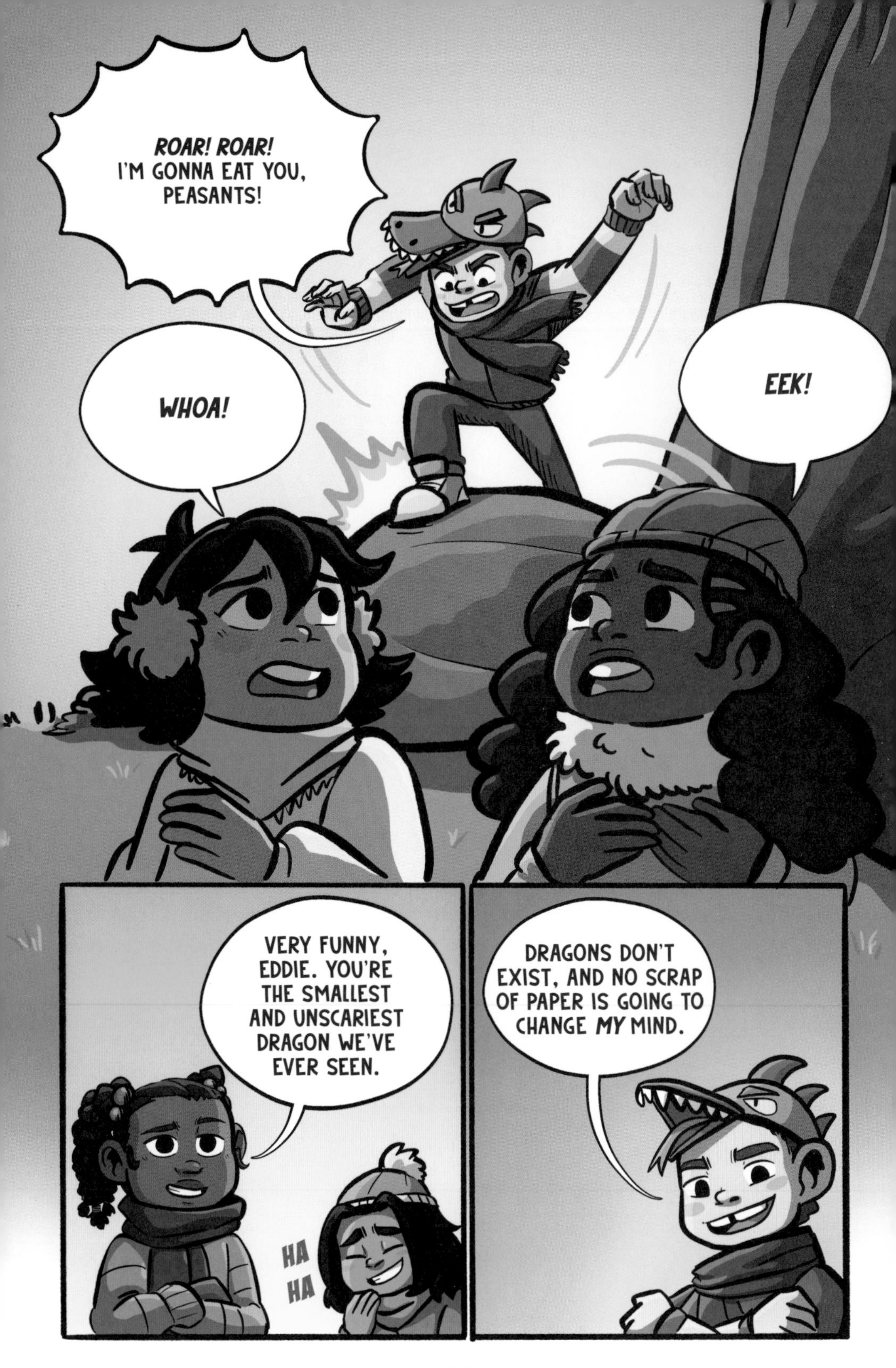
ROAR! ROAR! I'M GONNA EAT YOU, PEASANTS!
WHOA!
EEK!
VERY FUNNY, EDDIE. YOU'RE THE SMALLEST AND UNSCARIEST DRAGON WE'VE EVER SEEN.
HA HA
DRAGONS DON'T EXIST, AND NO SCRAP OF PAPER IS GOING TO CHANGE MY MIND.

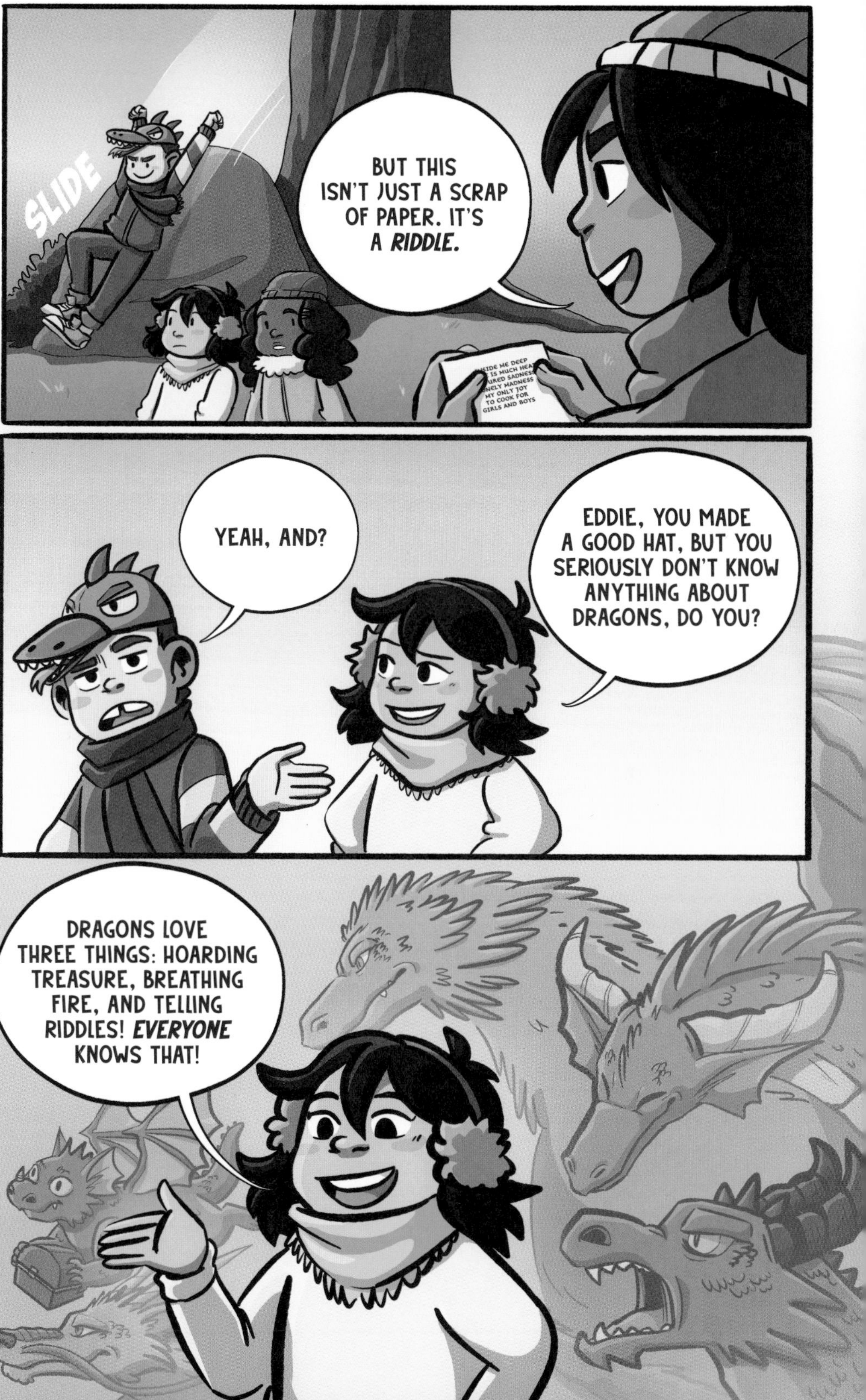
SLIDE
BUT THIS ISN'T JUST A SCRAP OF PAPER. IT'S A *RIDDLE.*
YEAH, AND?
EDDIE, YOU MADE A GOOD HAT, BUT YOU SERIOUSLY DON'T KNOW ANYTHING ABOUT DRAGONS, DO YOU?
DRAGONS LOVE THREE THINGS: HOARDING TREASURE, BREATHING FIRE, AND TELLING RIDDLES! *EVERYONE* KNOWS THAT!

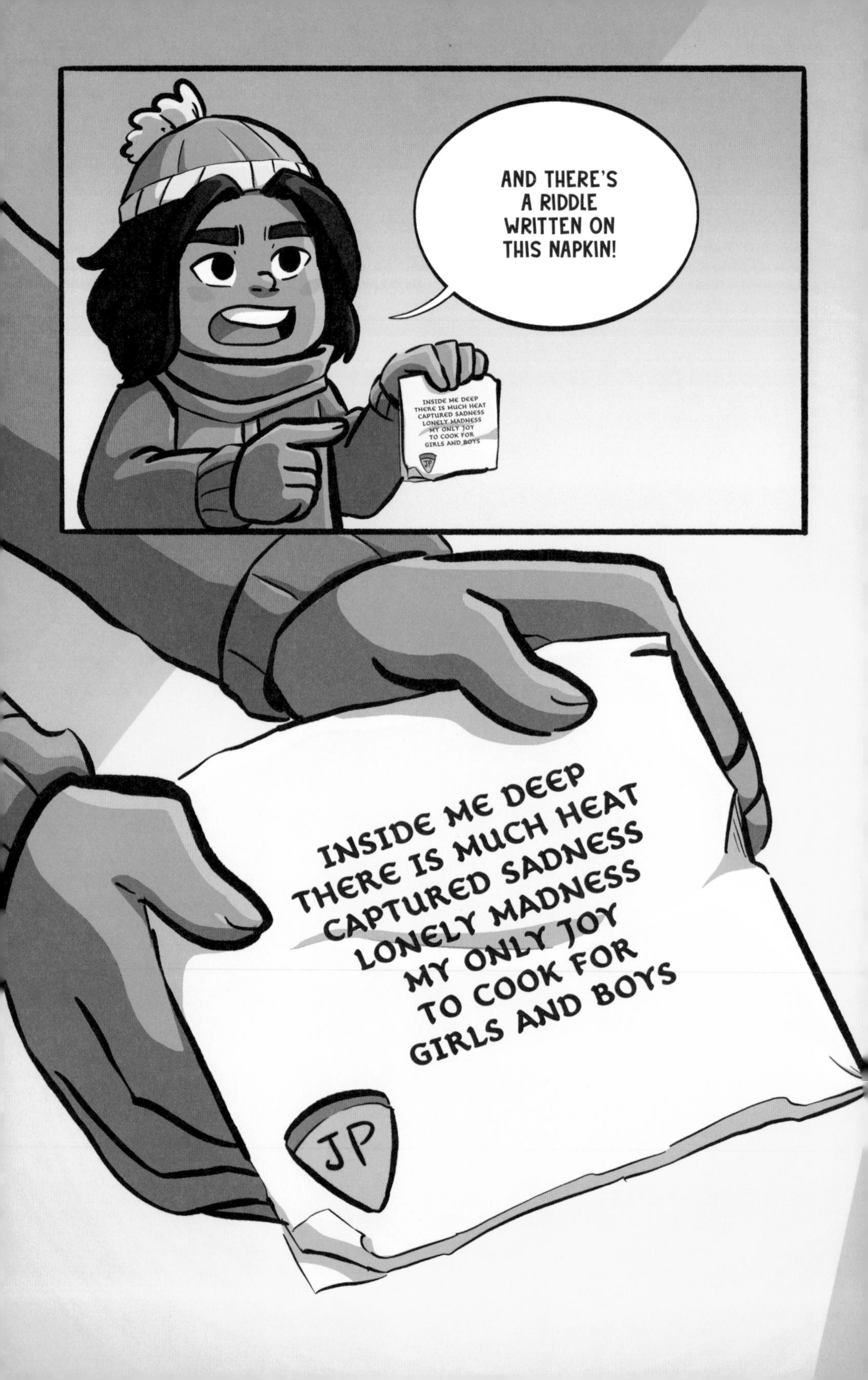
AND THERE'S A RIDDLE WRITTEN ON THIS NAPKIN!
INSIDE ME DEEP
THERE IS MUCH HEAT
CAPTURED SADNESS
LONELY MADNESS
MY ONLY JOY
TO COOK FOR
GIRLS AND BOYS
JP
INSIDE ME DEEP
THERE IS MUCH HEAT
CAPTURED SADNESS
LONELY MADNESS
MY ONLY JOY
TO COOK FOR
GIRLS AND BOYS
JP

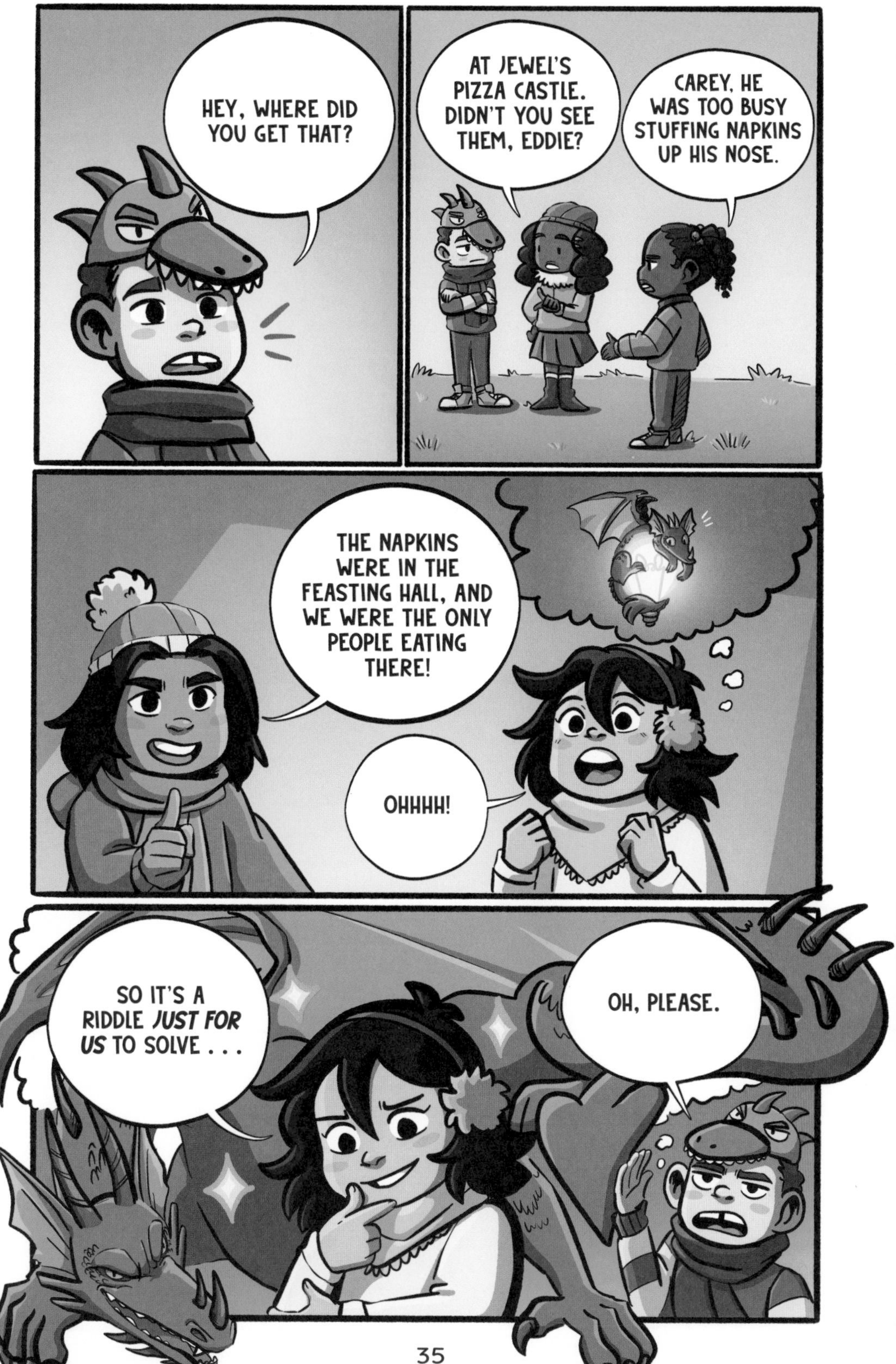
HEY, WHERE DID YOU GET THAT?
AT JEWEL'S PIZZA CASTLE. DIDN'T YOU SEE THEM, EDDIE?
CAREY, HE WAS TOO BUSY STUFFING NAPKINS UP HIS NOSE.
THE NAPKINS WERE IN THE FEASTING HALL, AND WE WERE THE ONLY PEOPLE EATING THERE!
OHHHH!
SO IT'S A RIDDLE *JUST FOR US* TO SOLVE . . .
OH, PLEASE.

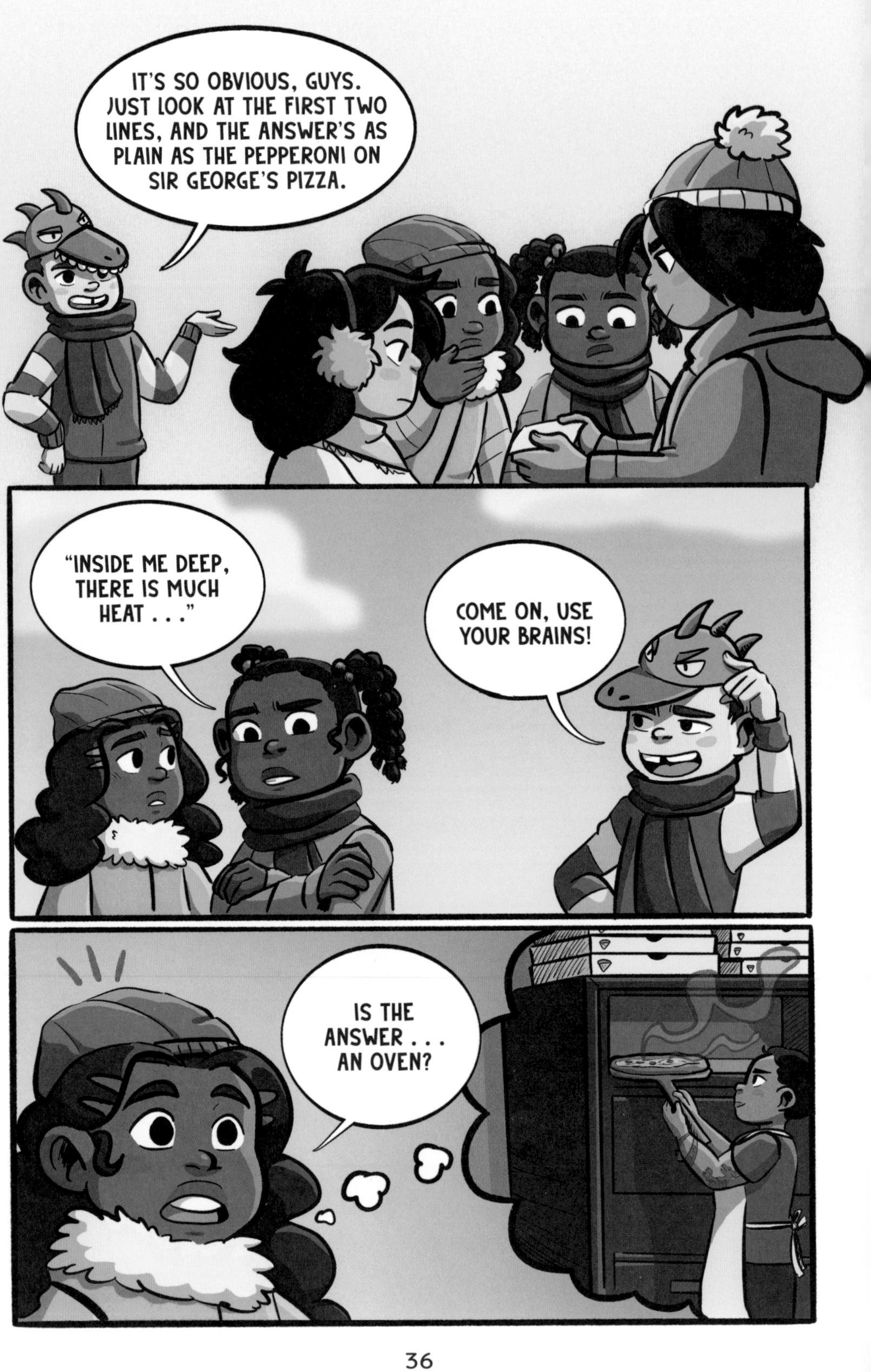
IT'S SO OBVIOUS, GUYS. JUST LOOK AT THE FIRST TWO LINES, AND THE ANSWER'S AS PLAIN AS THE PEPPERONI ON SIR GEORGE'S PIZZA.
"INSIDE ME DEEP, THERE IS MUCH HEAT . . ."
COME ON, USE YOUR BRAINS!
IS THE ANSWER . . . AN OVEN?

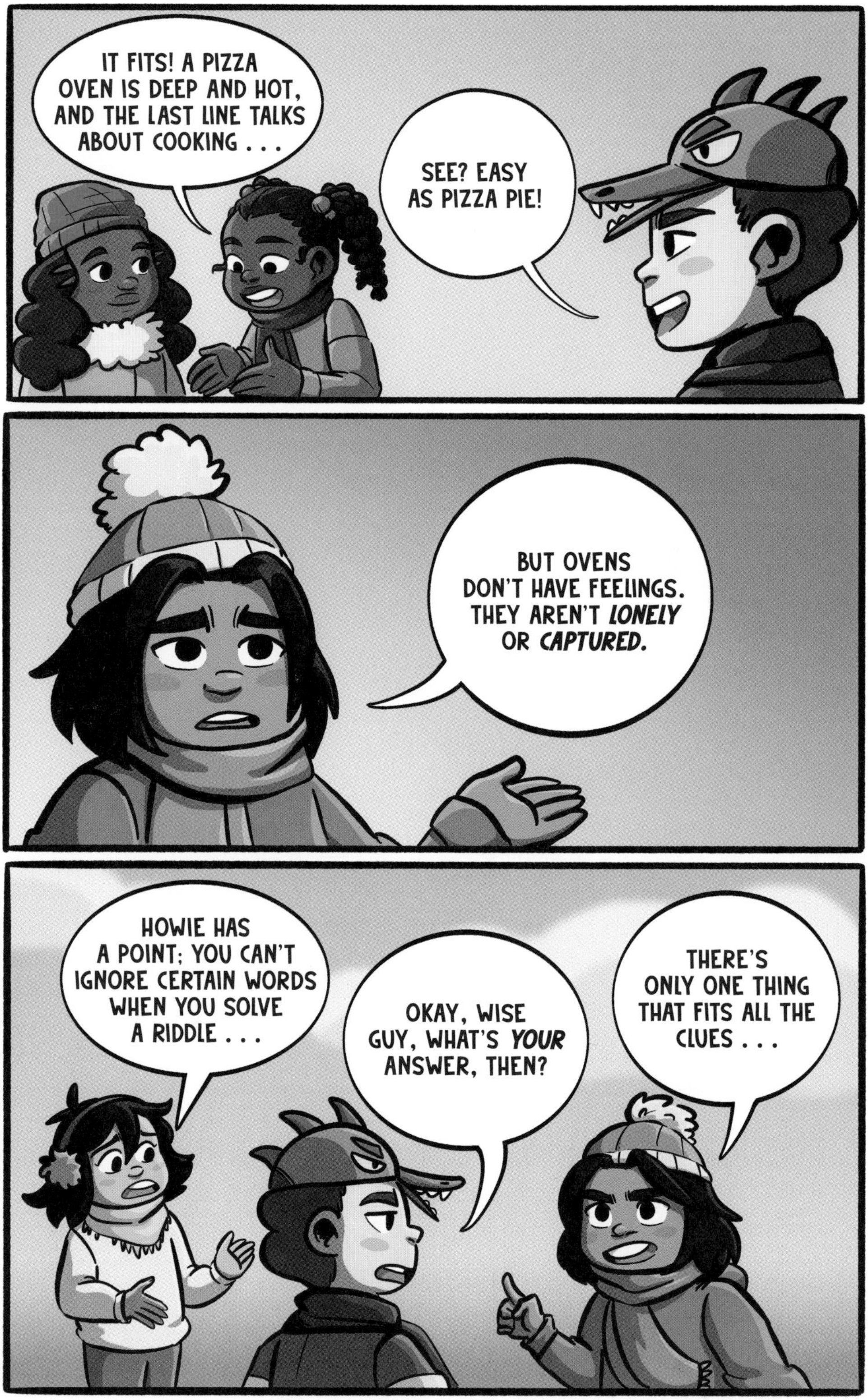
IT FITS! A PIZZA OVEN IS DEEP AND HOT, AND THE LAST LINE TALKS ABOUT COOKING . . .
SEE? EASY AS PIZZA PIE!
BUT OVENS DON'T HAVE FEELINGS. THEY AREN'T *LONELY* OR *CAPTURED.*
HOWIE HAS A POINT; YOU CAN'T IGNORE CERTAIN WORDS WHEN YOU SOLVE A RIDDLE . . .
OKAY, WISE GUY, WHAT'S *YOUR* ANSWER, THEN?
THERE'S ONLY ONE THING THAT FITS ALL THE CLUES . . .

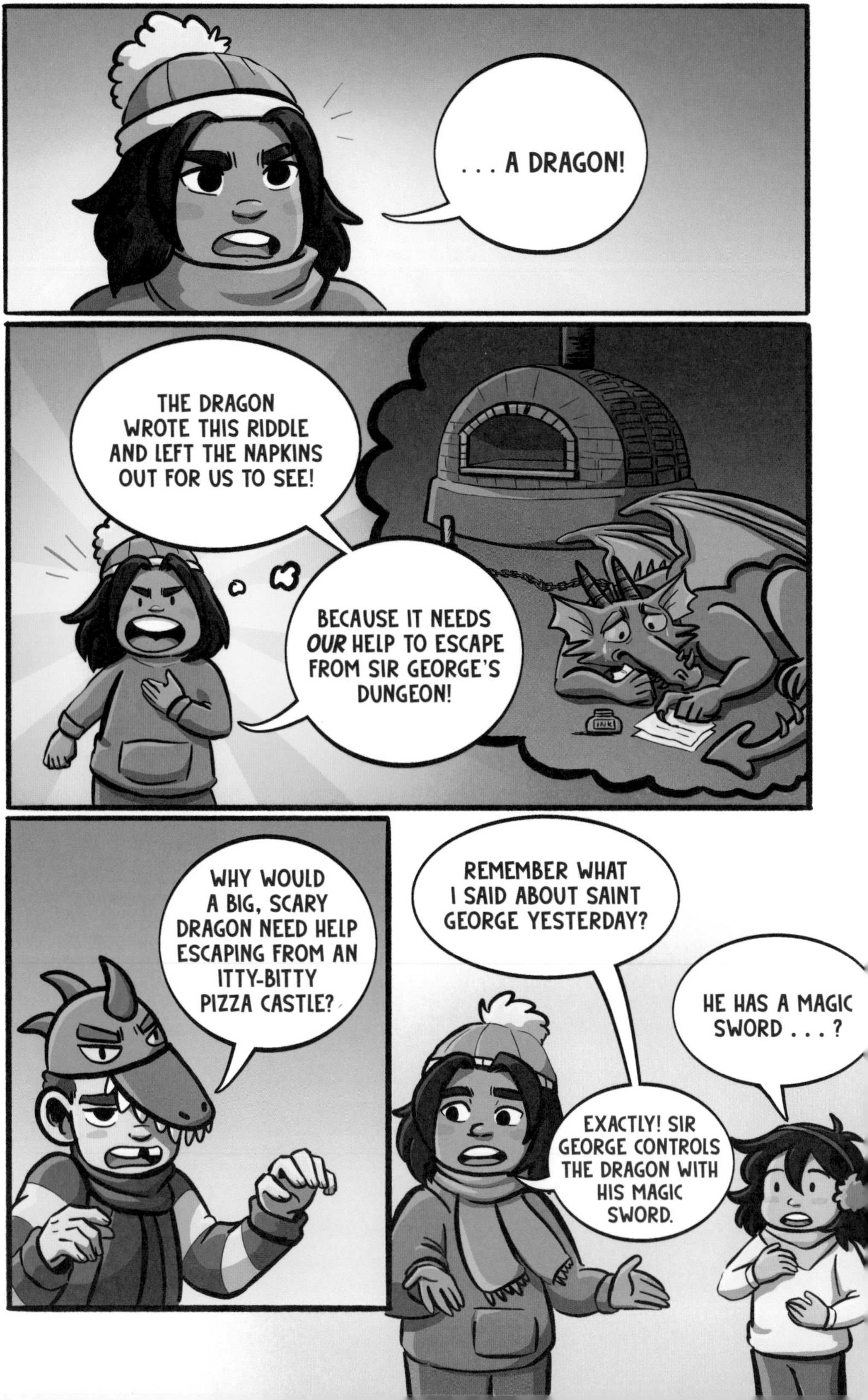
. . . A DRAGON!
THE DRAGON WROTE THIS RIDDLE AND LEFT THE NAPKINS OUT FOR US TO SEE!
BECAUSE IT NEEDS *OUR* HELP TO ESCAPE FROM SIR GEORGE'S DUNGEON!
INK
WHY WOULD A BIG, SCARY DRAGON NEED HELP ESCAPING FROM AN ITTY-BITTY PIZZA CASTLE?
REMEMBER WHAT I SAID ABOUT SAINT GEORGE YESTERDAY?
HE HAS A MAGIC SWORD . . . ?
EXACTLY! SIR GEORGE CONTROLS THE DRAGON WITH HIS MAGIC SWORD.

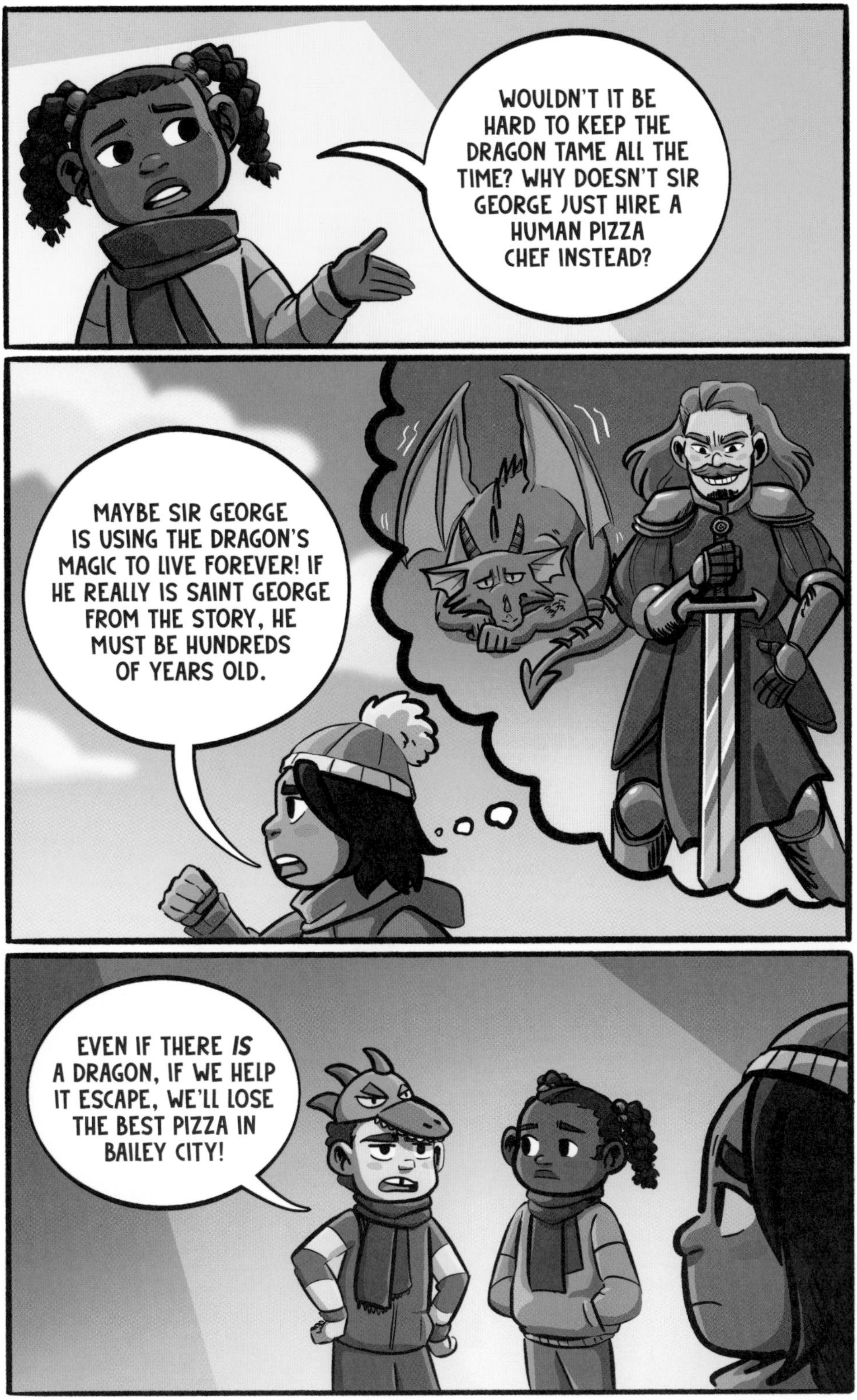
WOULDN'T IT BE HARD TO KEEP THE DRAGON TAME ALL THE TIME? WHY DOESN'T SIR GEORGE JUST HIRE A HUMAN PIZZA CHEF INSTEAD?
MAYBE SIR GEORGE IS USING THE DRAGON'S MAGIC TO LIVE FOREVER! IF HE REALLY IS SAINT GEORGE FROM THE STORY, HE MUST BE HUNDREDS OF YEARS OLD.
EVEN IF THERE *IS* A DRAGON, IF WE HELP IT ESCAPE, WE'LL LOSE THE BEST PIZZA IN BAILEY CITY!

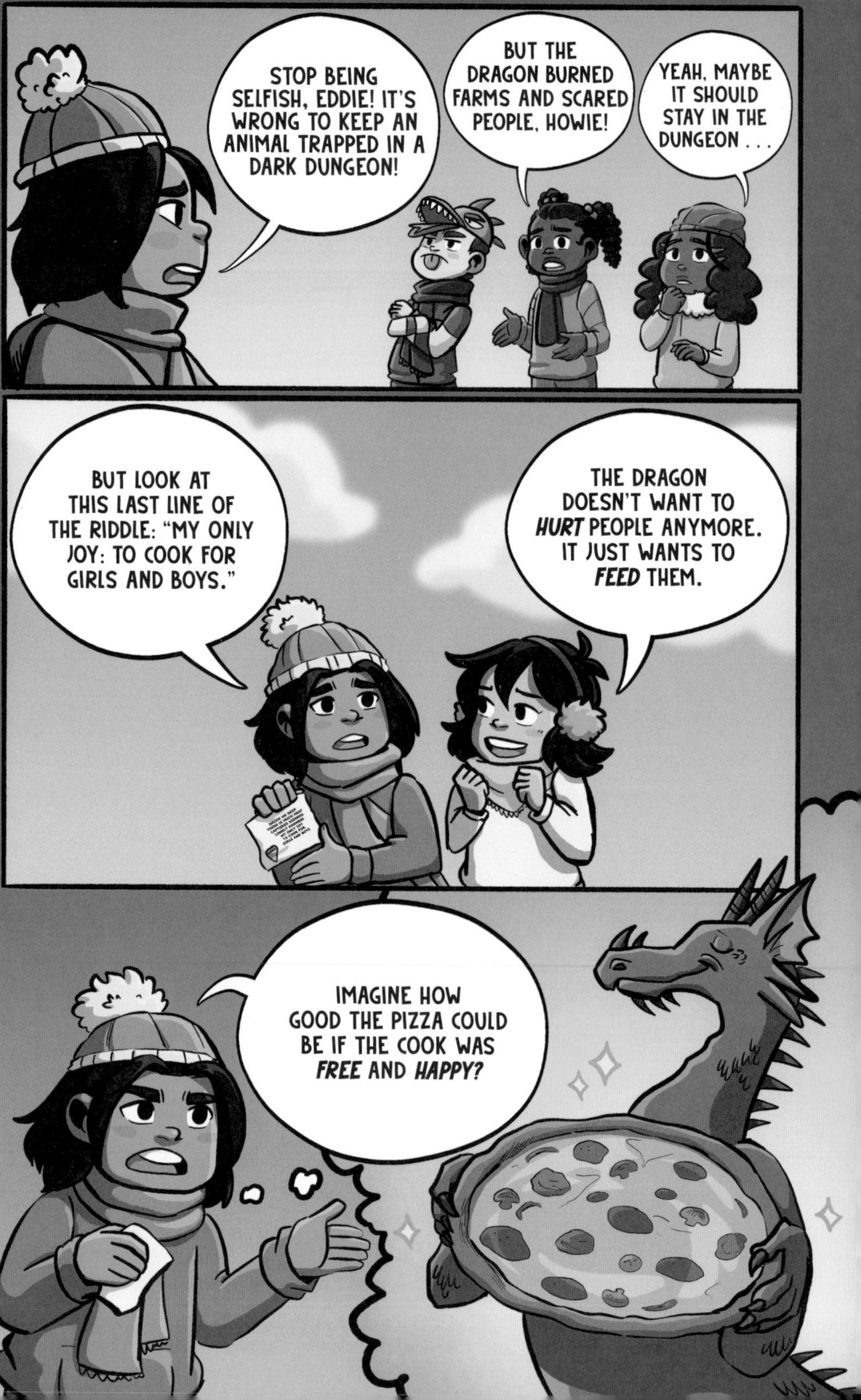
STOP BEING SELFISH, EDDIE! IT'S WRONG TO KEEP AN ANIMAL TRAPPED IN A DARK DUNGEON!
BUT THE DRAGON BURNED FARMS AND SCARED PEOPLE, HOWIE!
YEAH, MAYBE IT SHOULD STAY IN THE DUNGEON . . .
BUT LOOK AT THIS LAST LINE OF THE RIDDLE: "MY ONLY JOY: TO COOK FOR GIRLS AND BOYS."
THE DRAGON DOESN'T WANT TO *HURT* PEOPLE ANYMORE. IT JUST WANTS TO *FEED* THEM.
IMAGINE HOW GOOD THE PIZZA COULD BE IF THE COOK WAS *FREE* AND *HAPPY?*

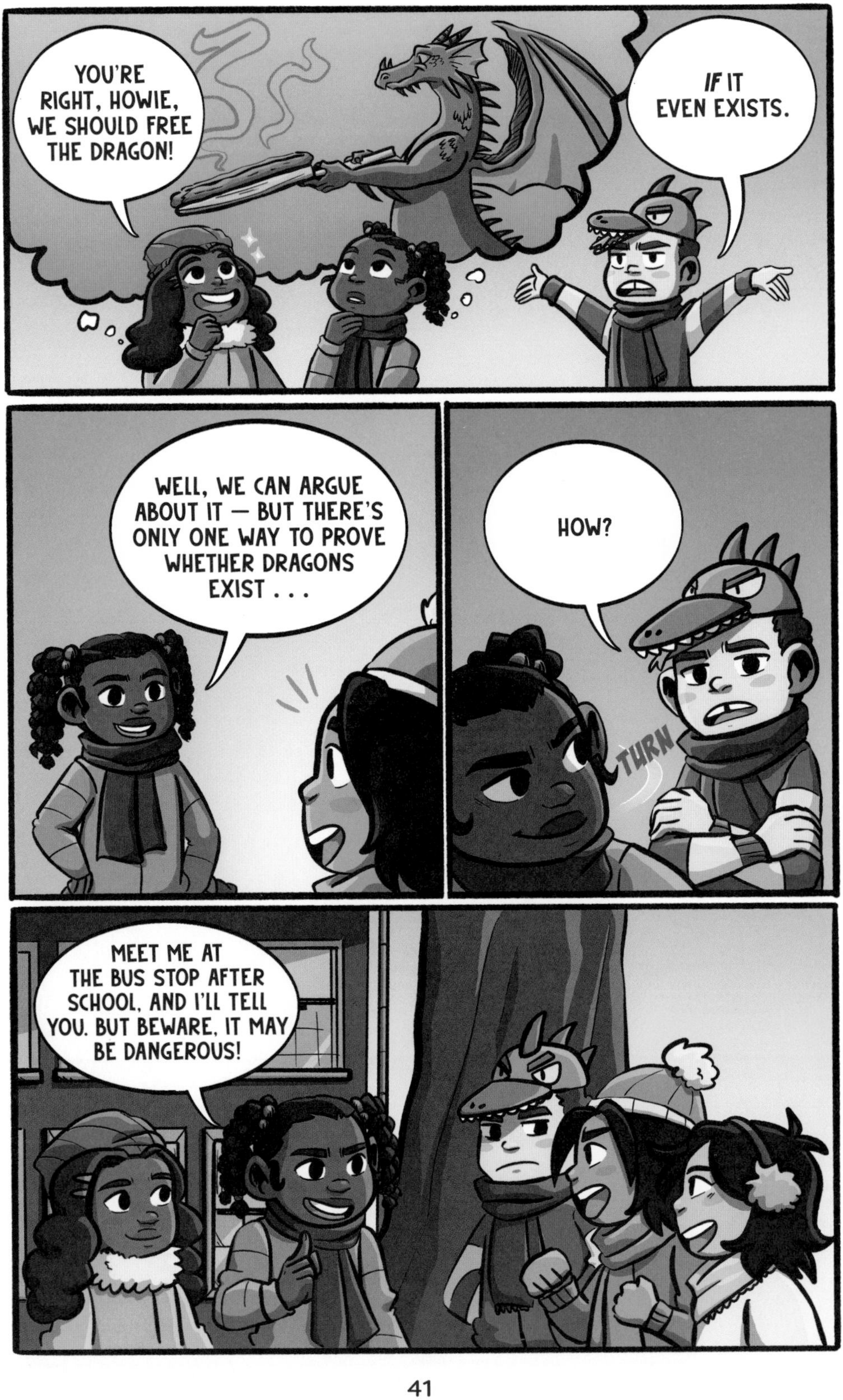
YOU'RE RIGHT, HOWIE, WE SHOULD FREE THE DRAGON!
IF IT EVEN EXISTS.
WELL, WE CAN ARGUE ABOUT IT — BUT THERE'S ONLY ONE WAY TO PROVE WHETHER DRAGONS EXIST . . .
HOW?
TURN
MEET ME AT THE BUS STOP AFTER SCHOOL, AND I'LL TELL YOU. BUT BEWARE, IT MAY BE DANGEROUS!

CHAPTER 4 INTO THE DUNGEON

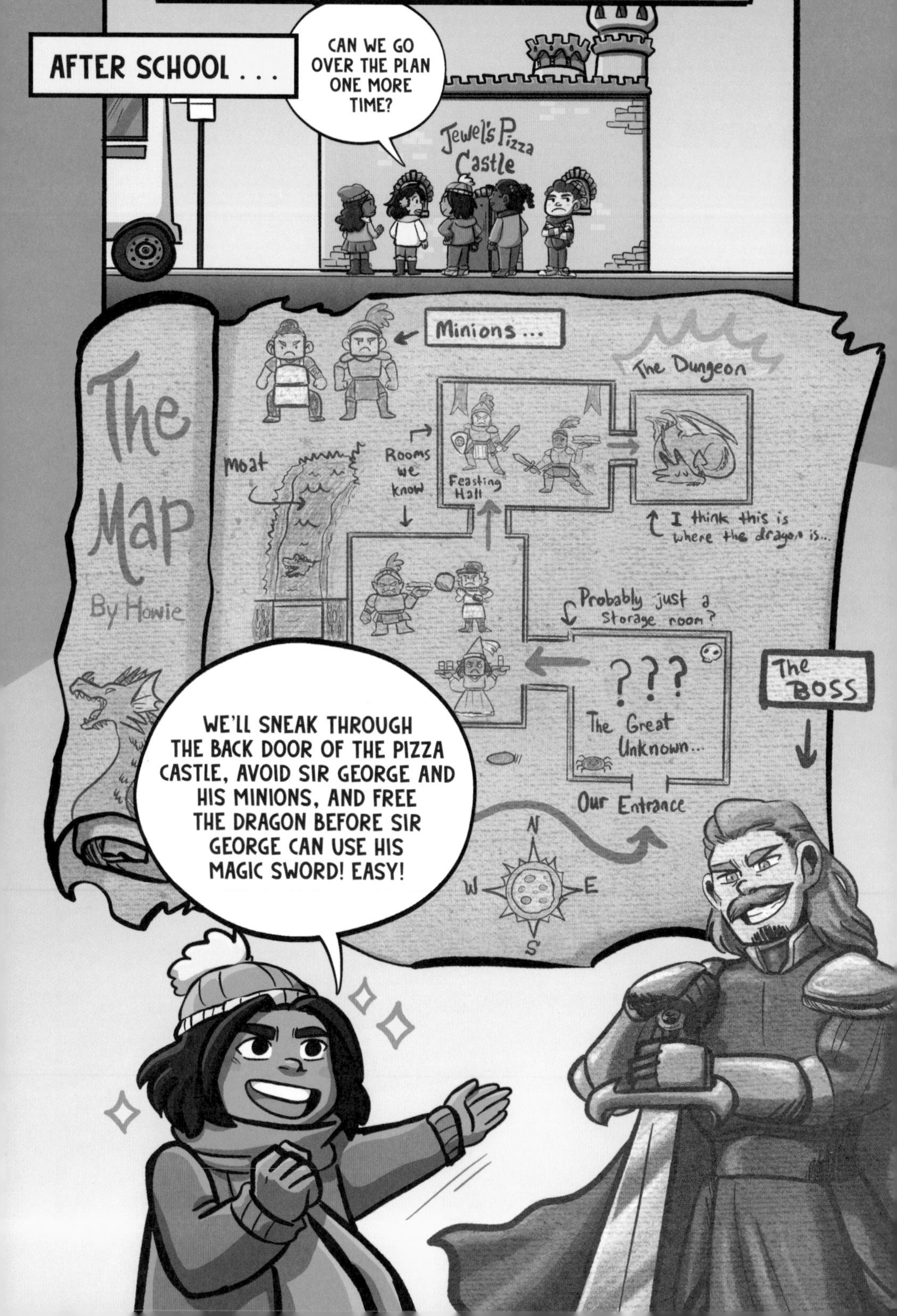
AFTER SCHOOL . . .
CAN WE GO OVER THE PLAN ONE MORE TIME?
Jewel's Pizza Castle
The Map
By Howie
Minions . . .
The Dungeon
moat
Rooms we know
Feasting Hall
I think this is where the dragon is...
Probably just a storage room?
??? The Great Unknown...
The BOSS
Our Entrance
N
W
E
S
WE'LL SNEAK THROUGH THE BACK DOOR OF THE PIZZA CASTLE, AVOID SIR GEORGE AND HIS MINIONS, AND FREE THE DRAGON BEFORE SIR GEORGE CAN USE HIS MAGIC SWORD! EASY!

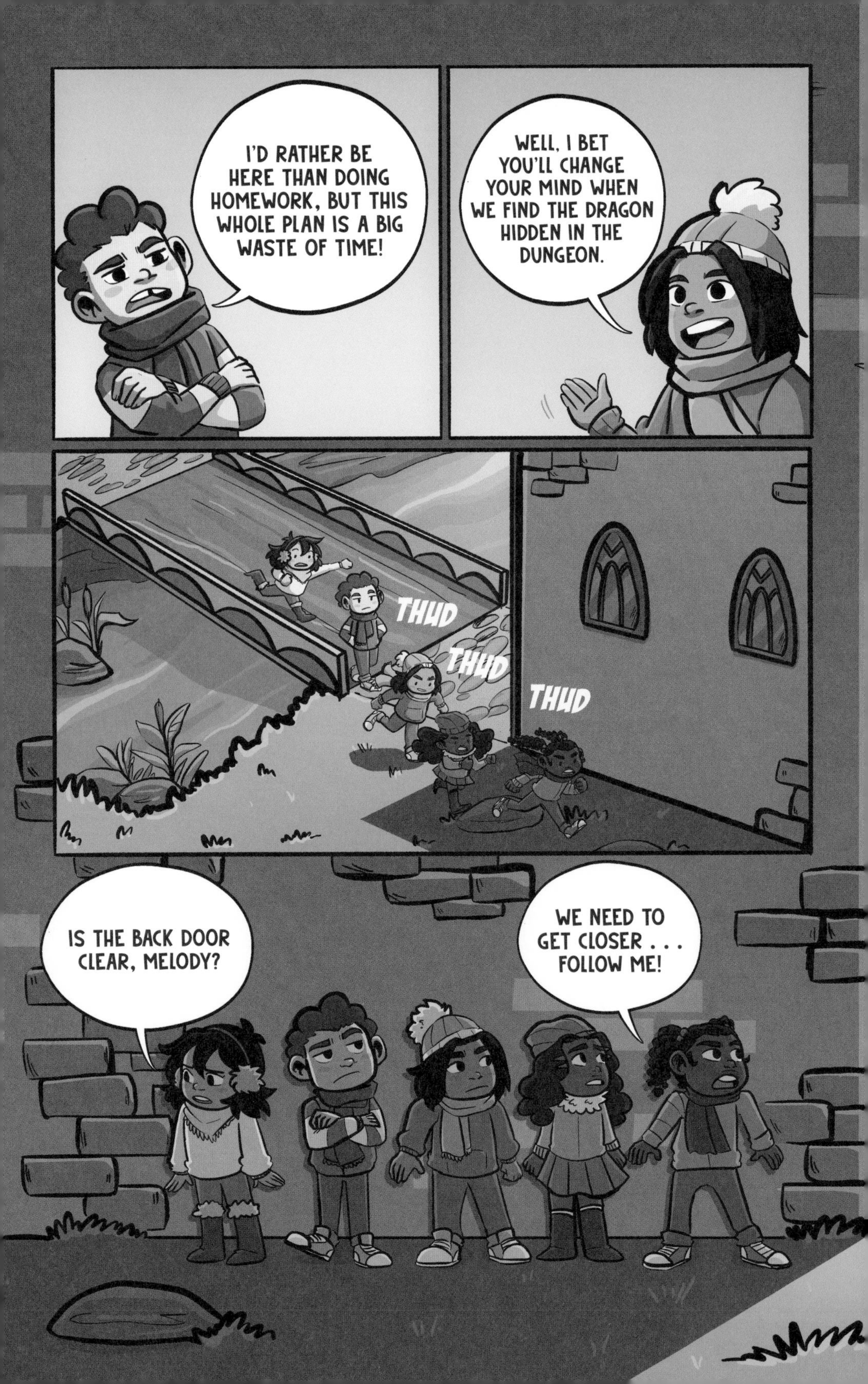
I'D RATHER BE HERE THAN DOING HOMEWORK, BUT THIS WHOLE PLAN IS A BIG WASTE OF TIME!
WELL, I BET YOU'LL CHANGE YOUR MIND WHEN WE FIND THE DRAGON HIDDEN IN THE DUNGEON.
THUD
THUD
THUD
IS THE BACK DOOR CLEAR, MELODY?
WE NEED TO GET CLOSER . . . FOLLOW ME!

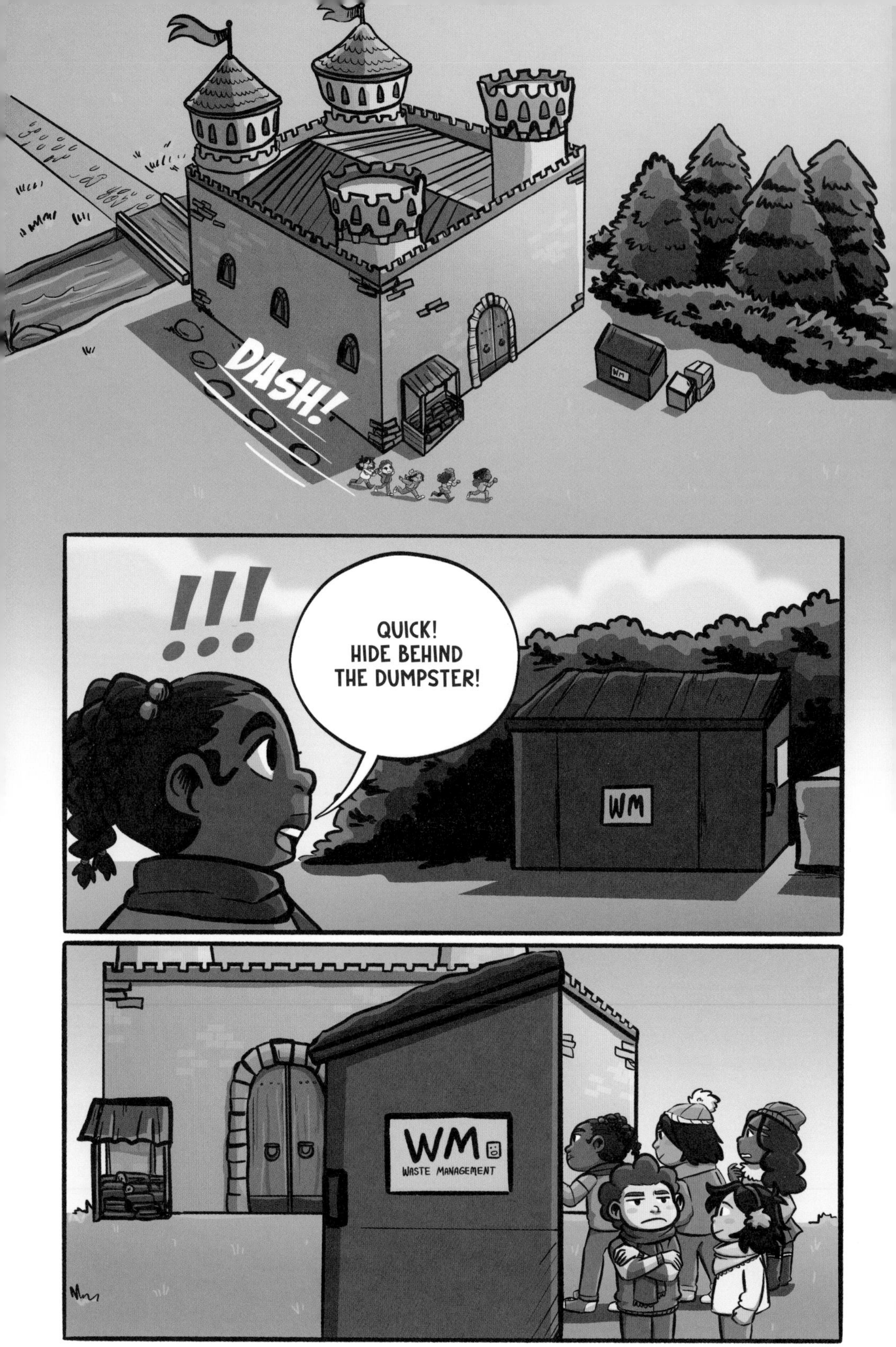
DASH!
!!!
QUICK! HIDE BEHIND THE DUMPSTER!
WM
WM
WASTE MANAGEMENT

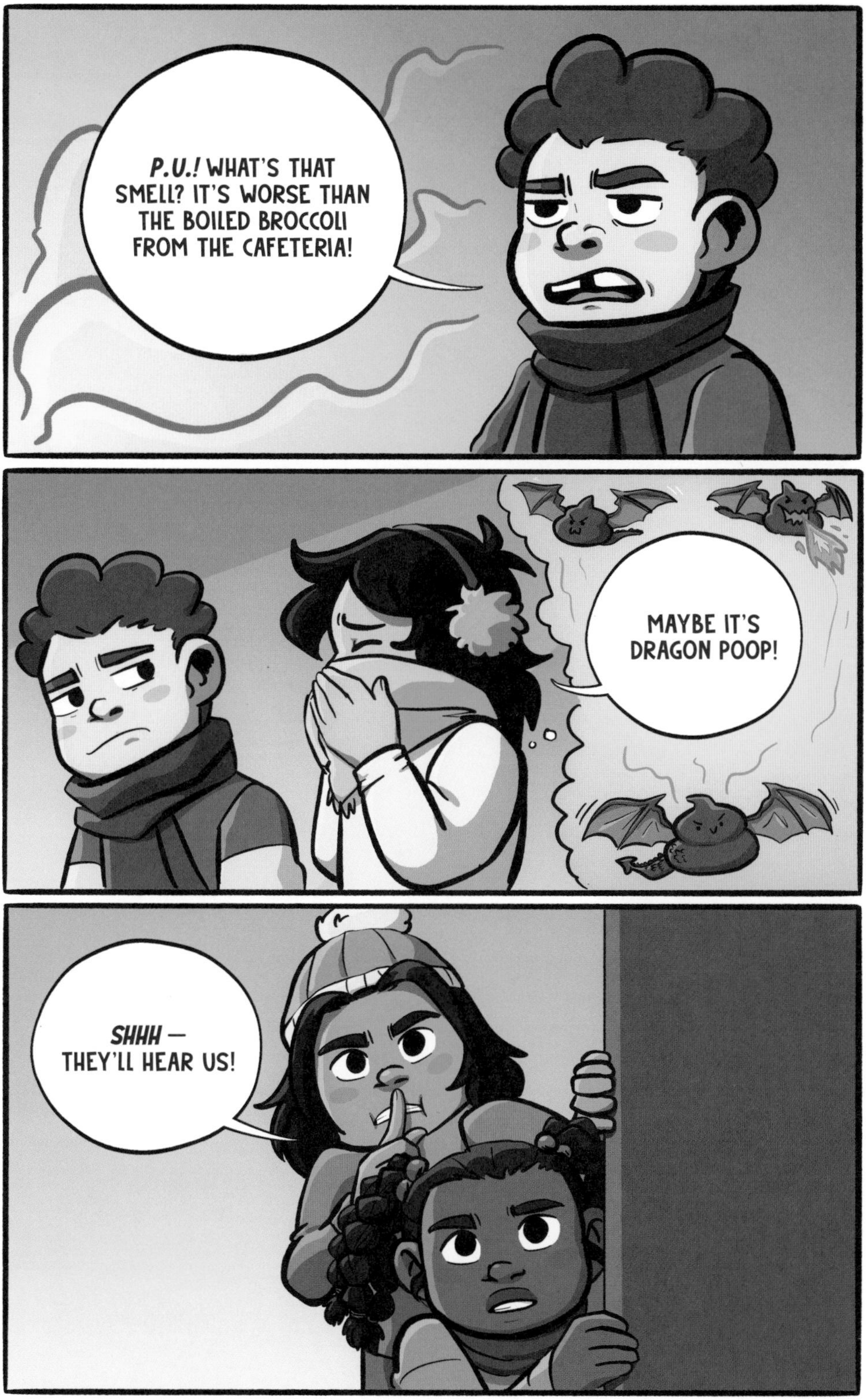
P.U.! WHAT'S THAT SMELL? IT'S WORSE THAN THE BOILED BROCCOLI FROM THE CAFETERIA!
MAYBE IT'S DRAGON POOP!
SHHH — THEY'LL HEAR US!

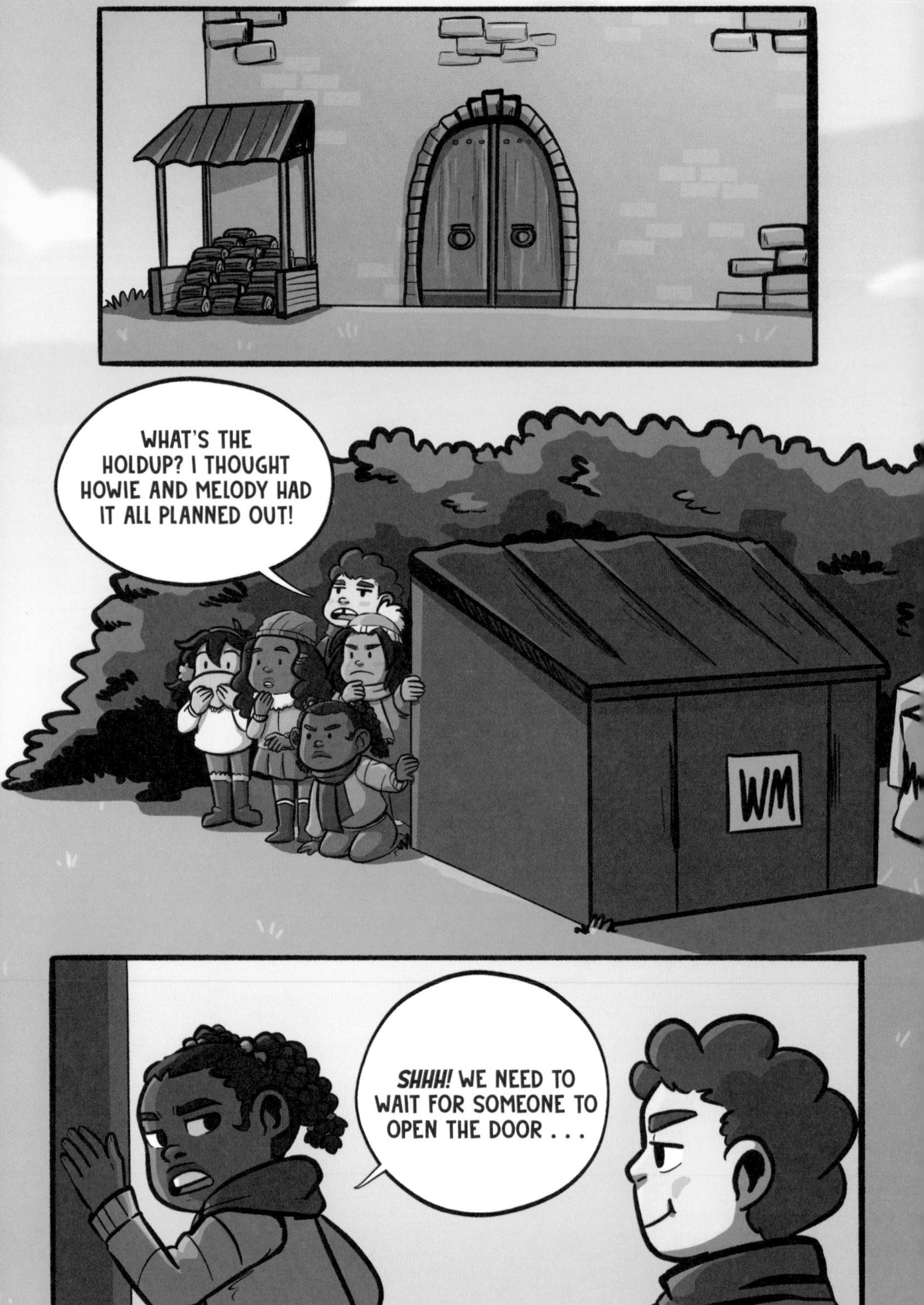
WM
WHAT'S THE HOLDUP? I THOUGHT HOWIE AND MELODY HAD IT ALL PLANNED OUT!
SHHH! WE NEED TO WAIT FOR SOMEONE TO OPEN THE DOOR . . .

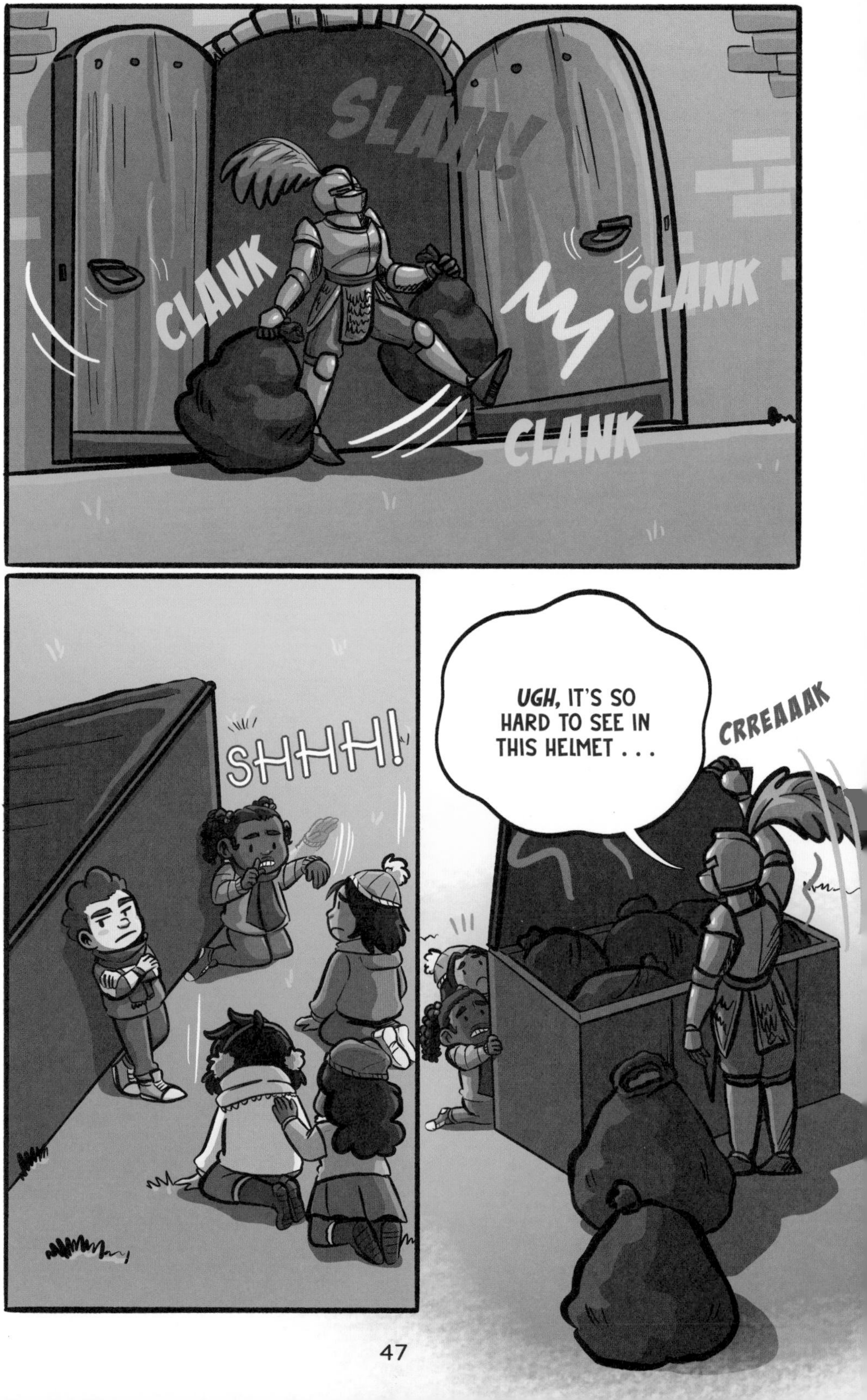
SLAM!
CLANK
CLANK
CLANK
SHHH!
UGH, IT'S SO HARD TO SEE IN THIS HELMET . . .
CRREAAAK

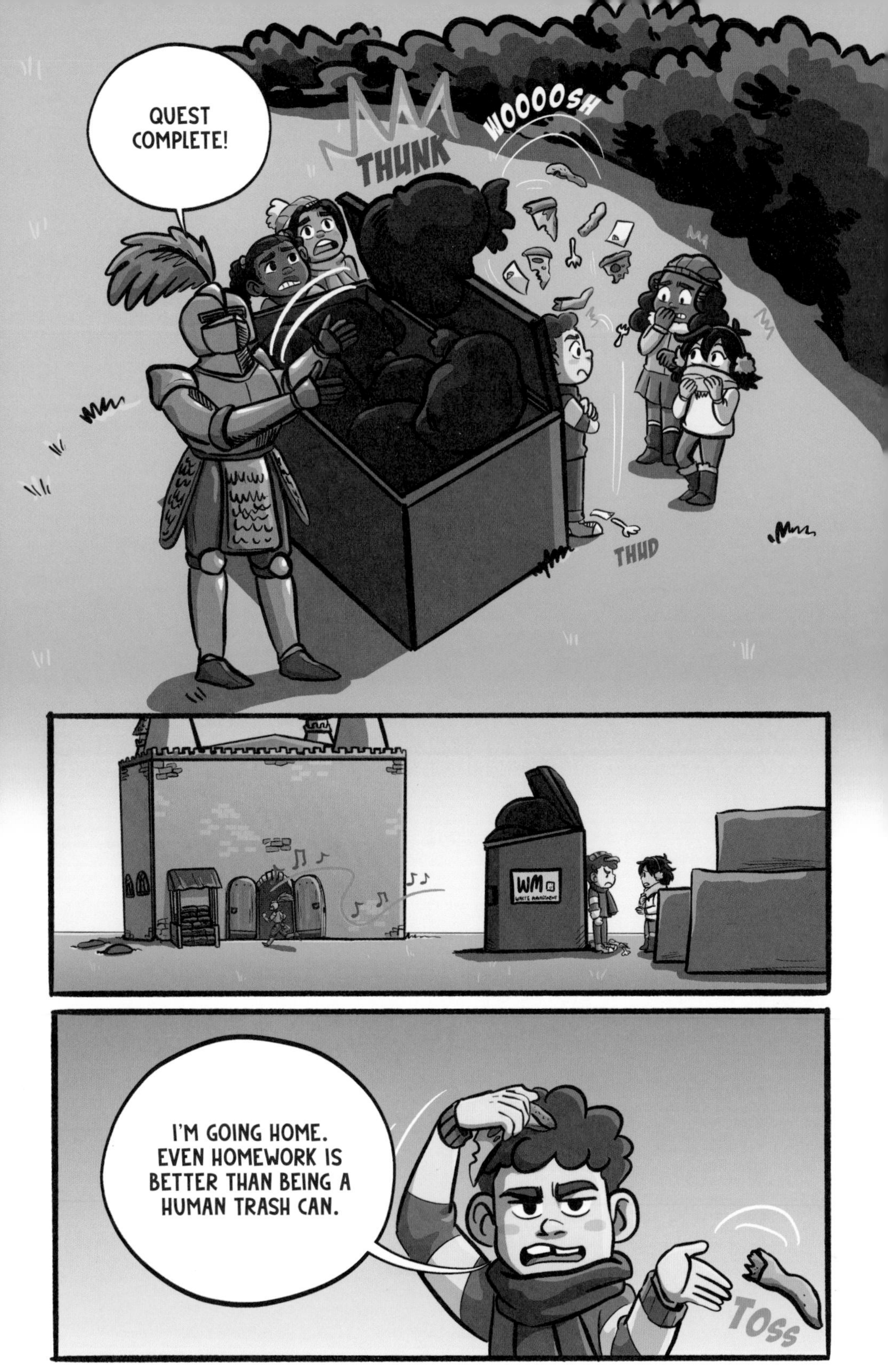
QUEST COMPLETE!
THUNK
WOOOOSH
THUD
I'M GOING HOME. EVEN HOMEWORK IS BETTER THAN BEING A HUMAN TRASH CAN.
TOSS

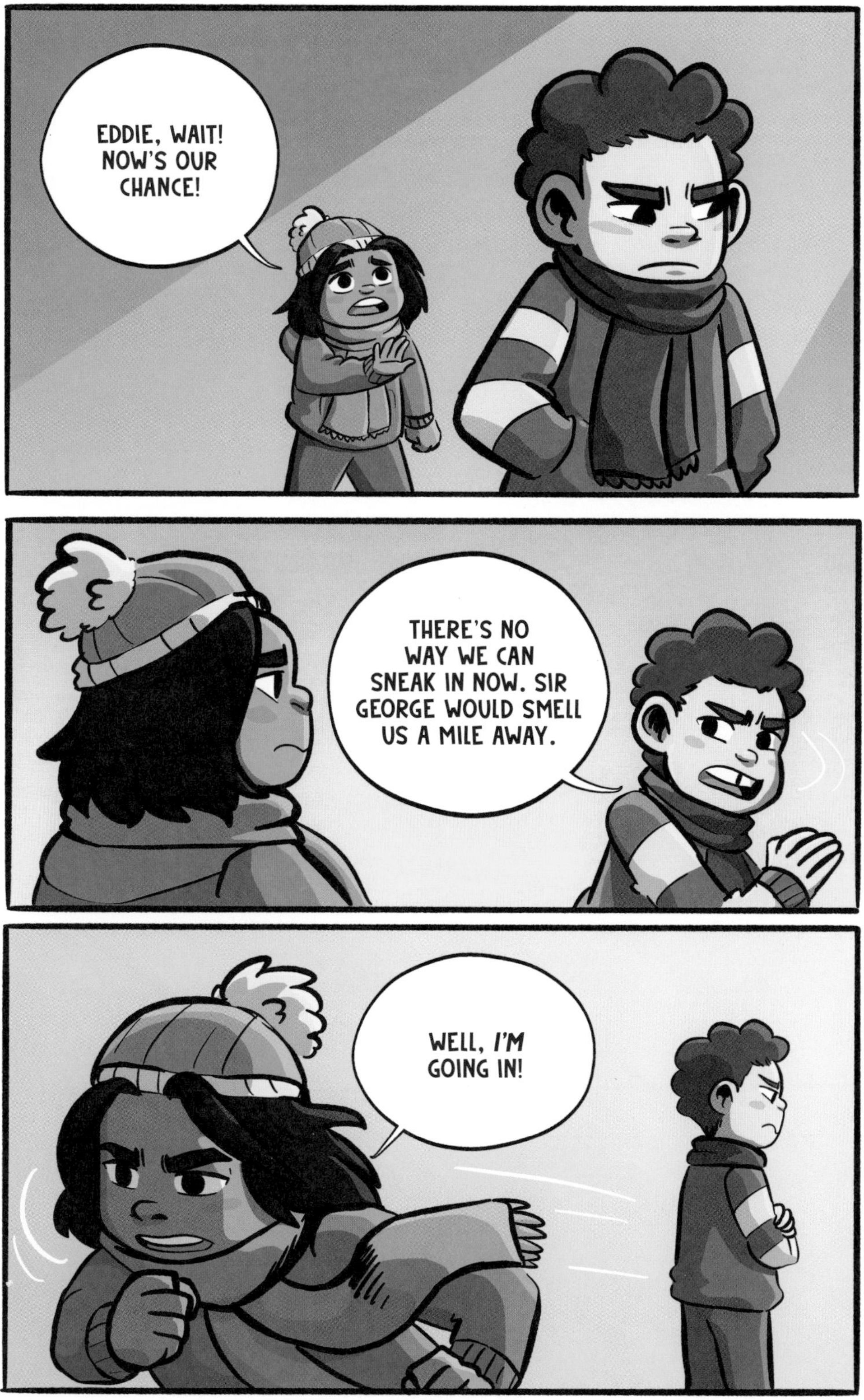
EDDIE, WAIT! NOW'S OUR CHANCE!
THERE'S NO WAY WE CAN SNEAK IN NOW. SIR GEORGE WOULD SMELL US A MILE AWAY.
WELL, *I'M* GOING IN!

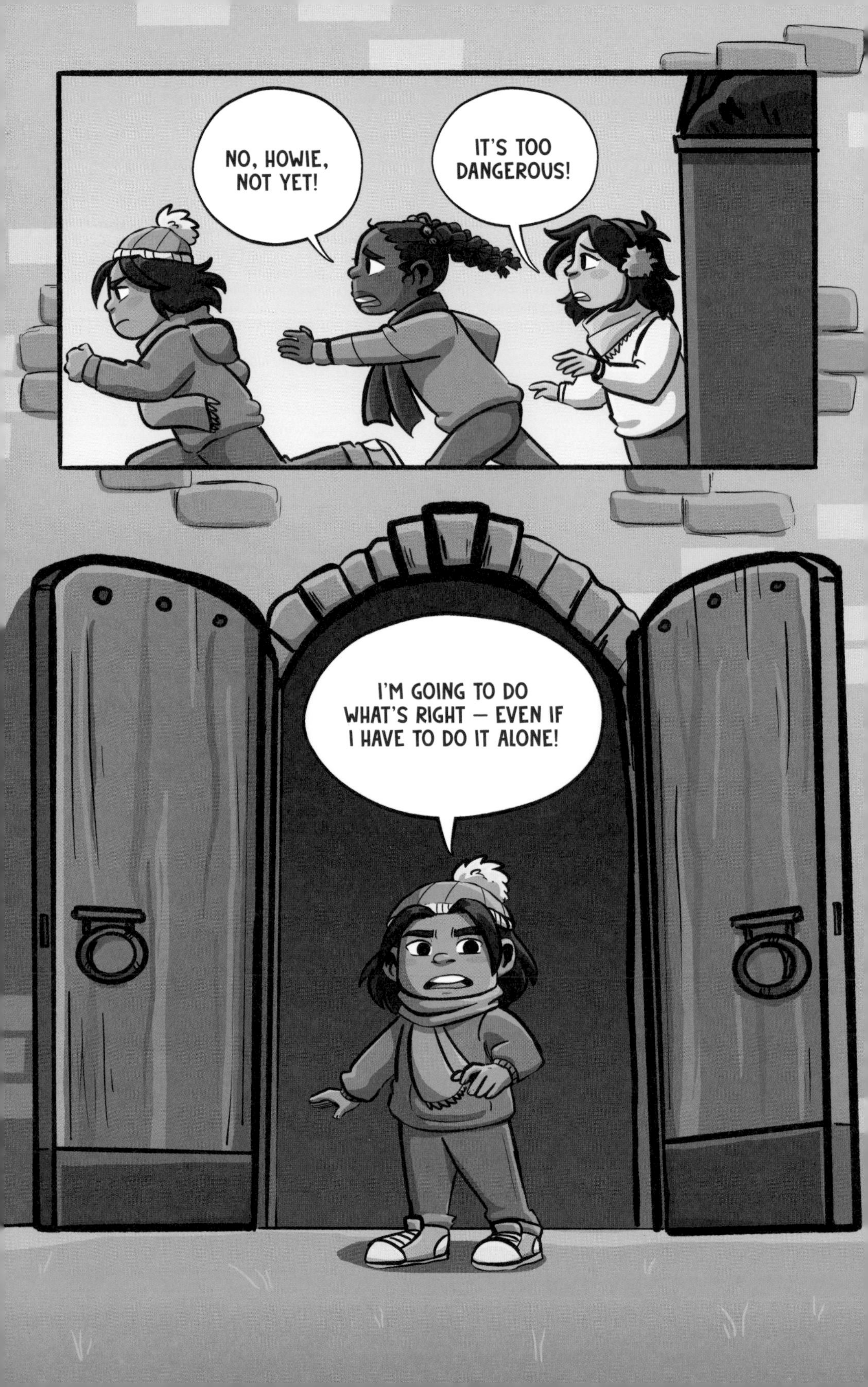
NO, HOWIE, NOT YET!
IT'S TOO DANGEROUS!
I'M GOING TO DO WHAT'S RIGHT — EVEN IF I HAVE TO DO IT ALONE!

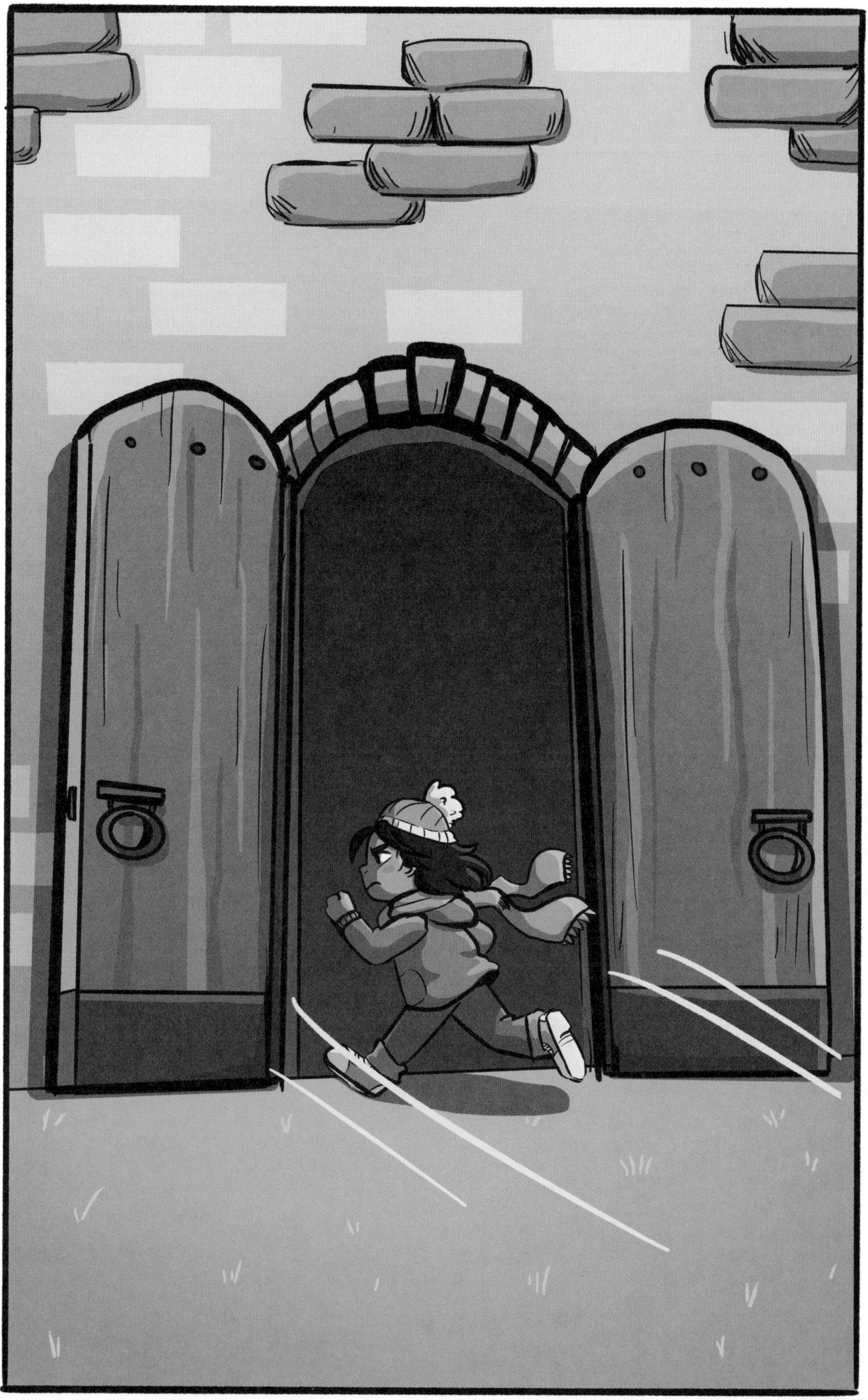

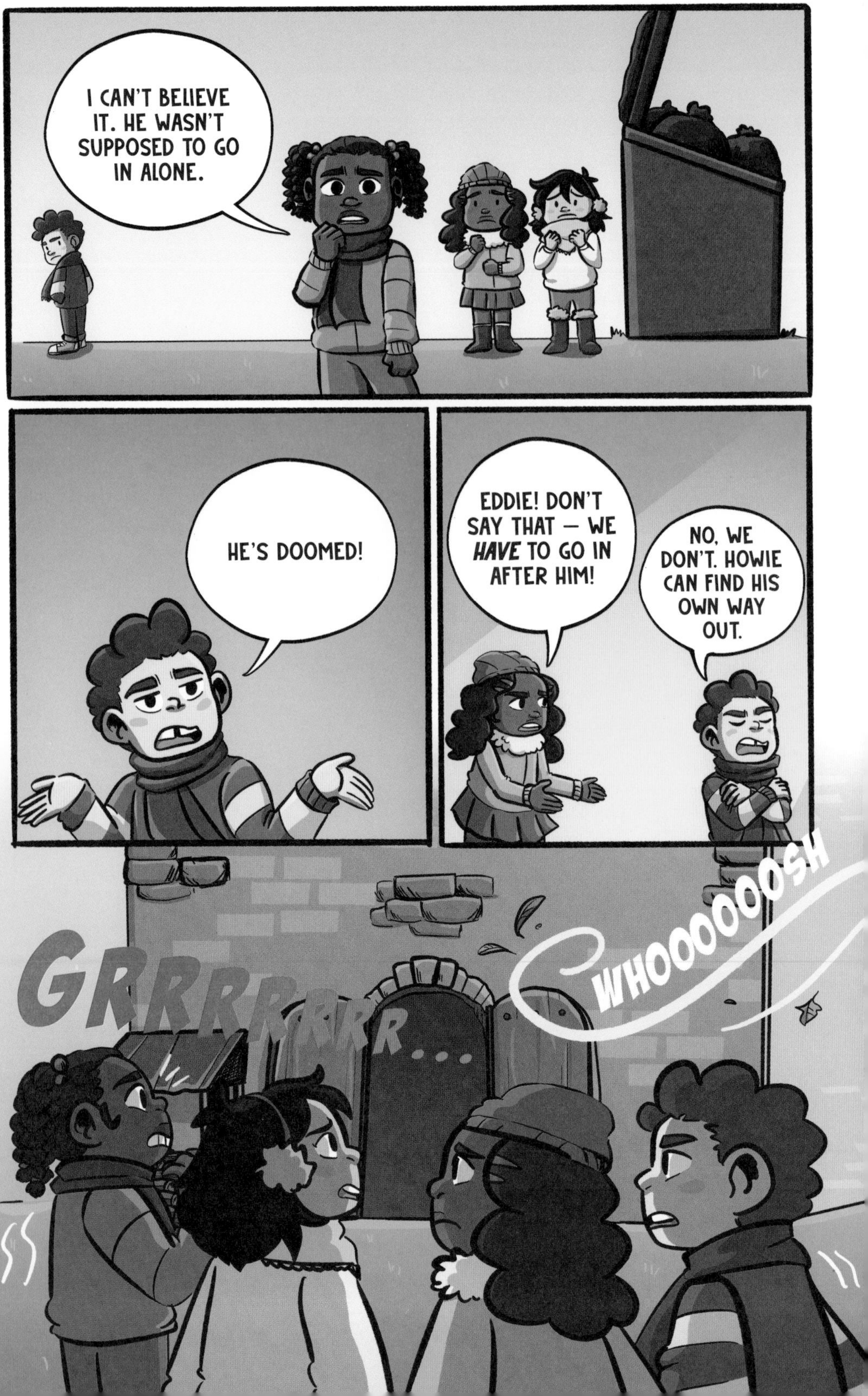
I CAN'T BELIEVE IT. HE WASN'T SUPPOSED TO GO IN ALONE.
HE'S DOOMED!
EDDIE! DON'T SAY THAT — WE *HAVE* TO GO IN AFTER HIM!
NO, WE DON'T. HOWIE CAN FIND HIS OWN WAY OUT.
GRRRRRRRR...
WHOOOOOOSH

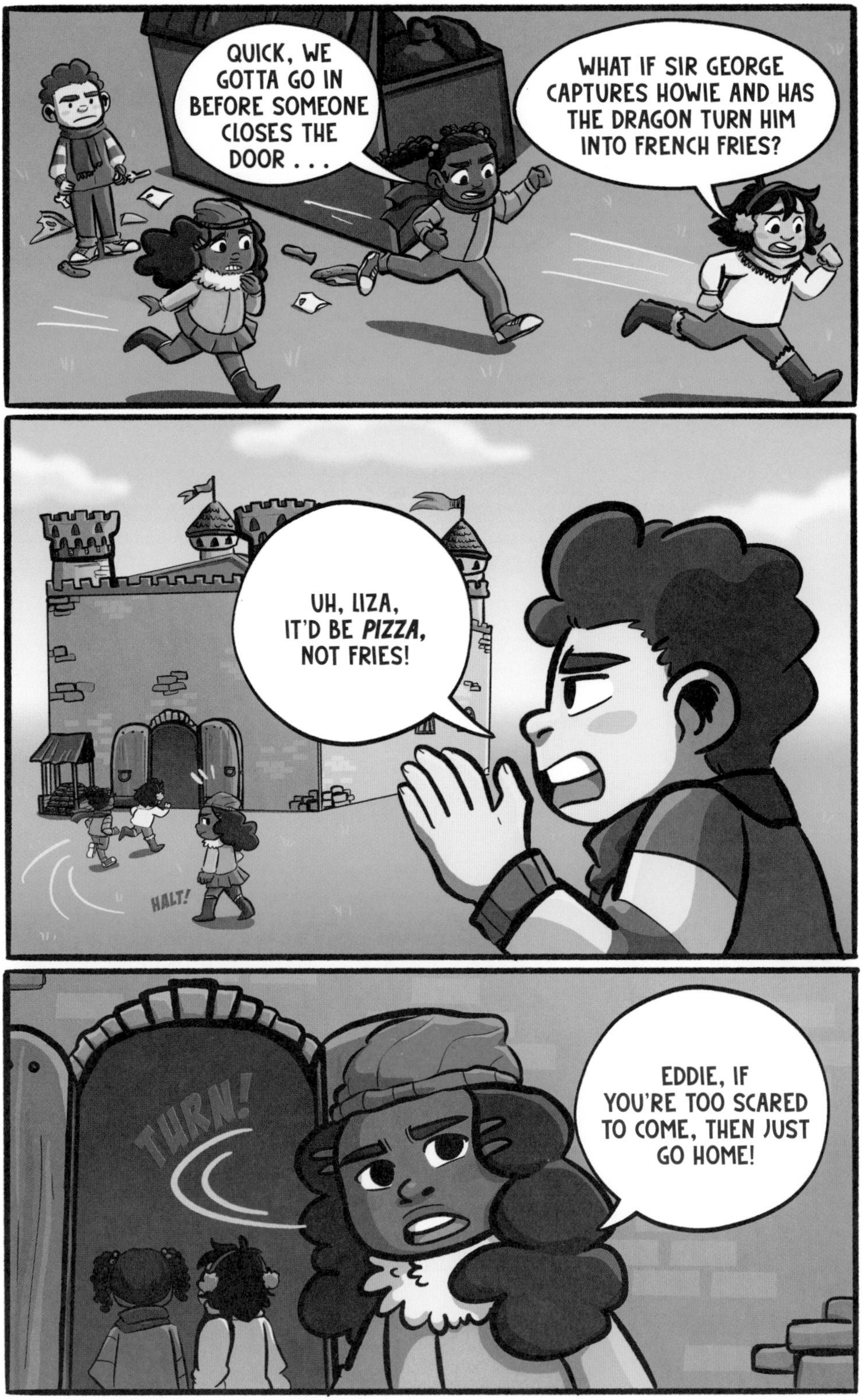
QUICK, WE GOTTA GO IN BEFORE SOMEONE CLOSES THE DOOR . . .
WHAT IF SIR GEORGE CAPTURES HOWIE AND HAS THE DRAGON TURN HIM INTO FRENCH FRIES?
UH, LIZA, IT'D BE *PIZZA*, NOT FRIES!
HALT!
TURN!
EDDIE, IF YOU'RE TOO SCARED TO COME, THEN JUST GO HOME!

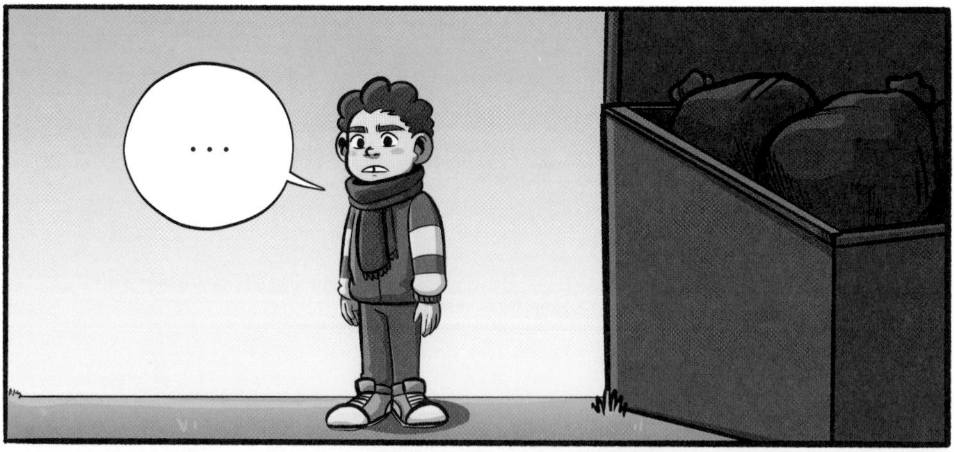
. . .

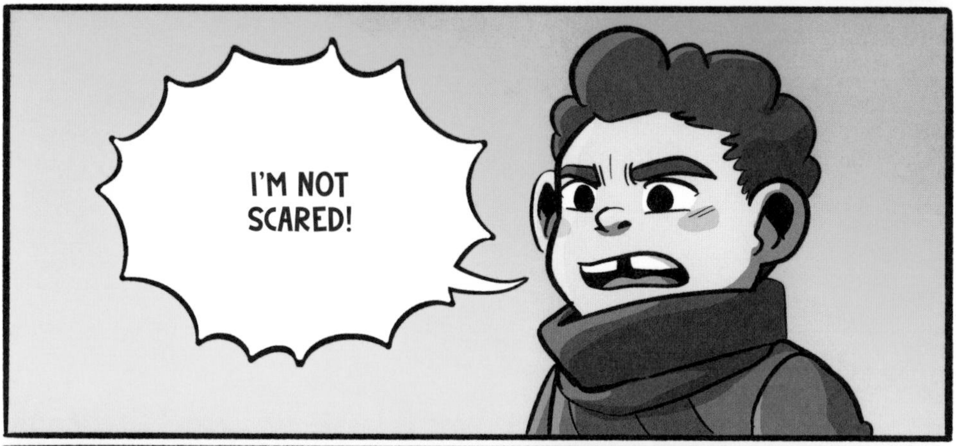
I'M NOT SCARED!

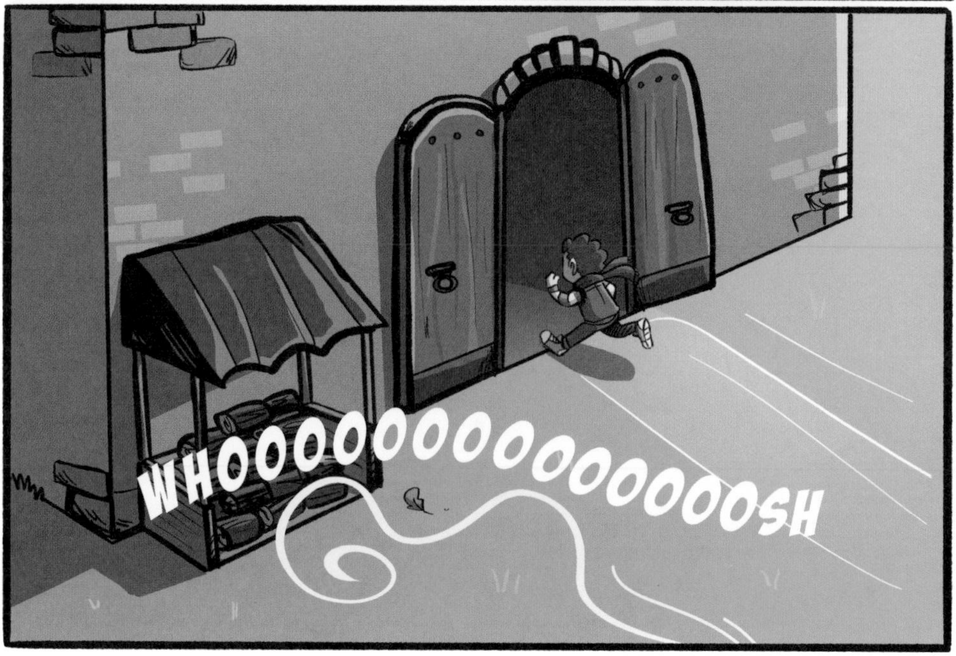
WHOOOOOOOOOOOOOOOSH

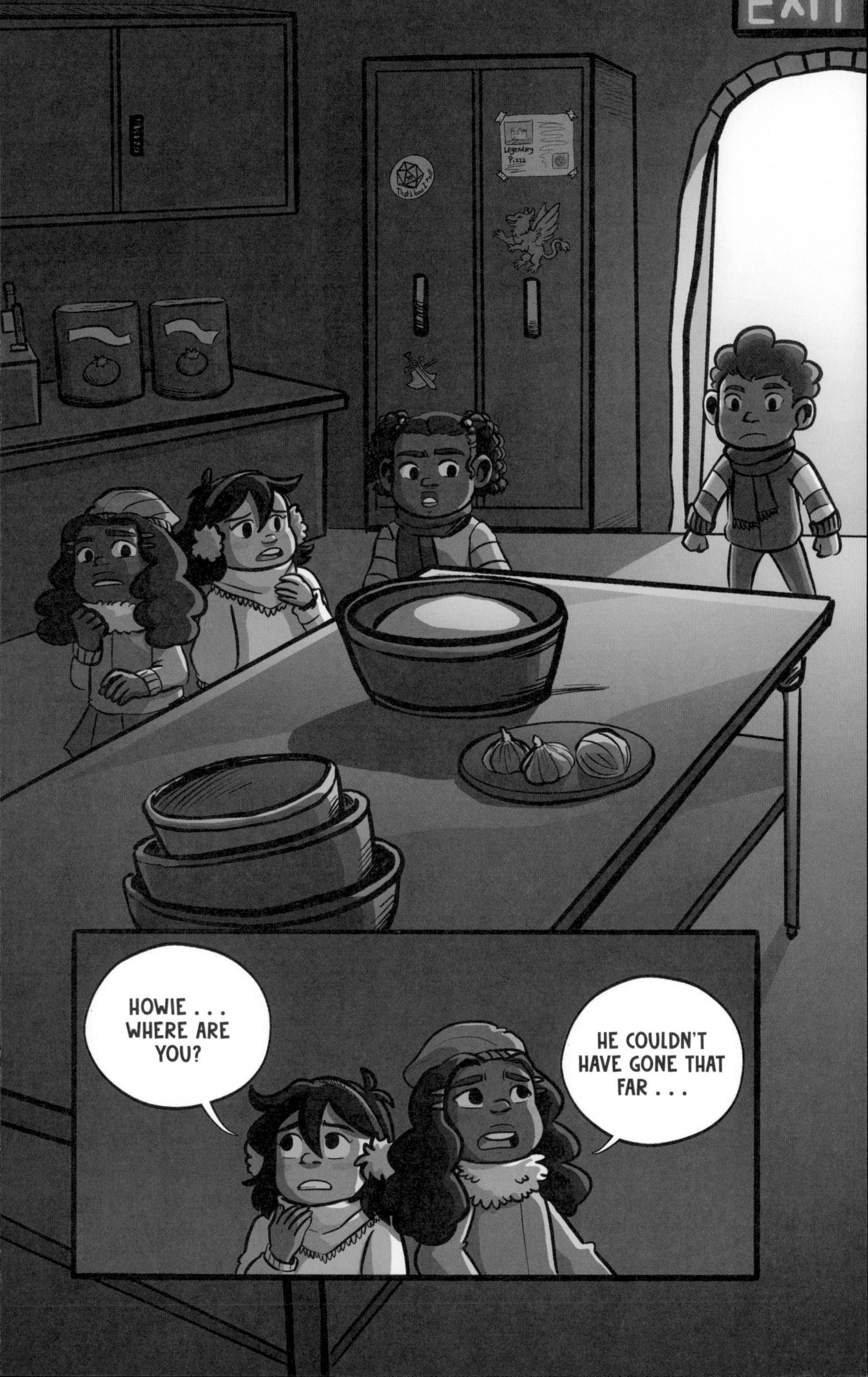

EXIT
That's how I roll
Legendary Pizza
HOWIE . . . WHERE ARE YOU?
HE COULDN'T HAVE GONE THAT FAR . . .

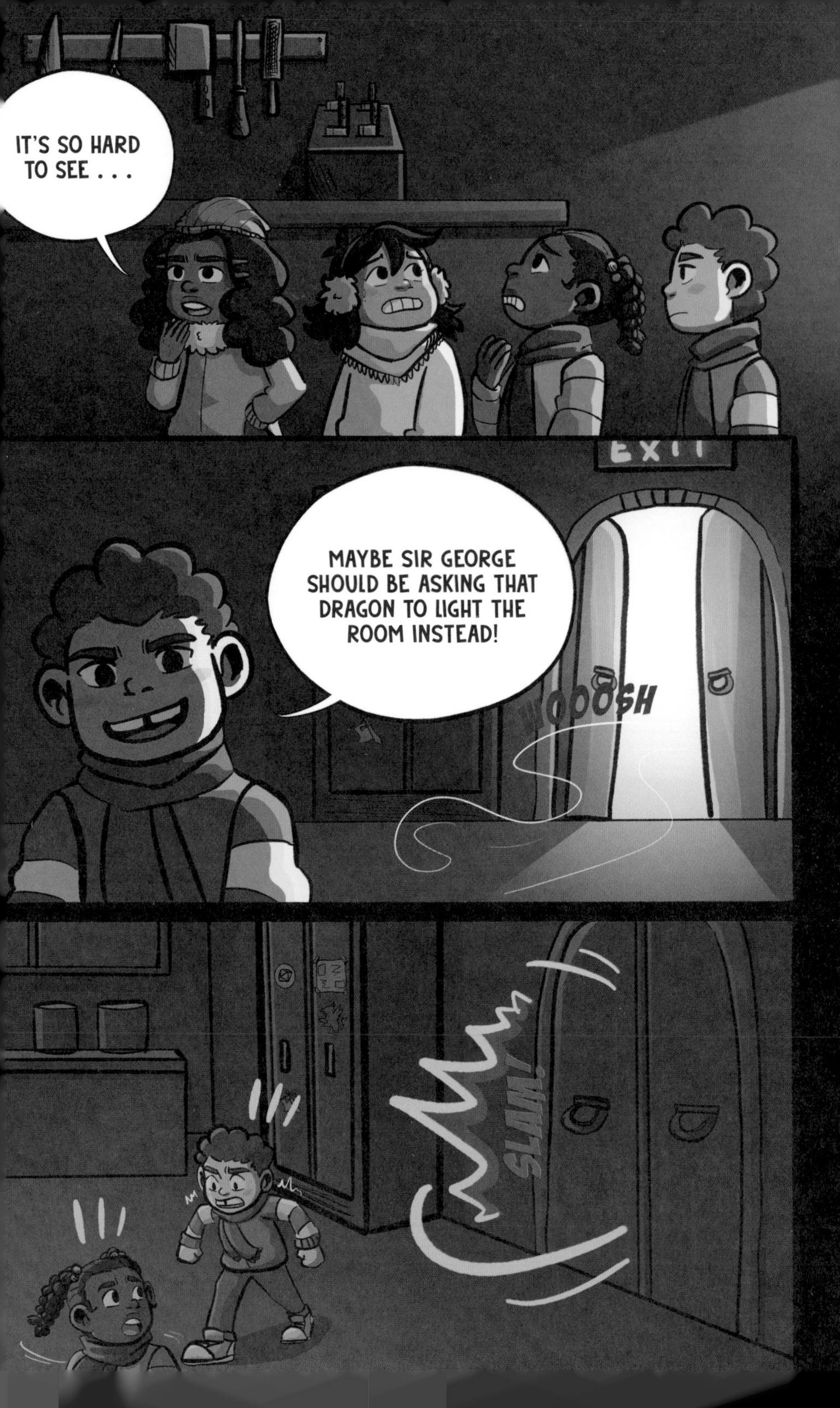
IT'S SO HARD TO SEE . . .
EXIT
MAYBE SIR GEORGE SHOULD BE ASKING THAT DRAGON TO LIGHT THE ROOM INSTEAD!
WOOOSH
SLAM!

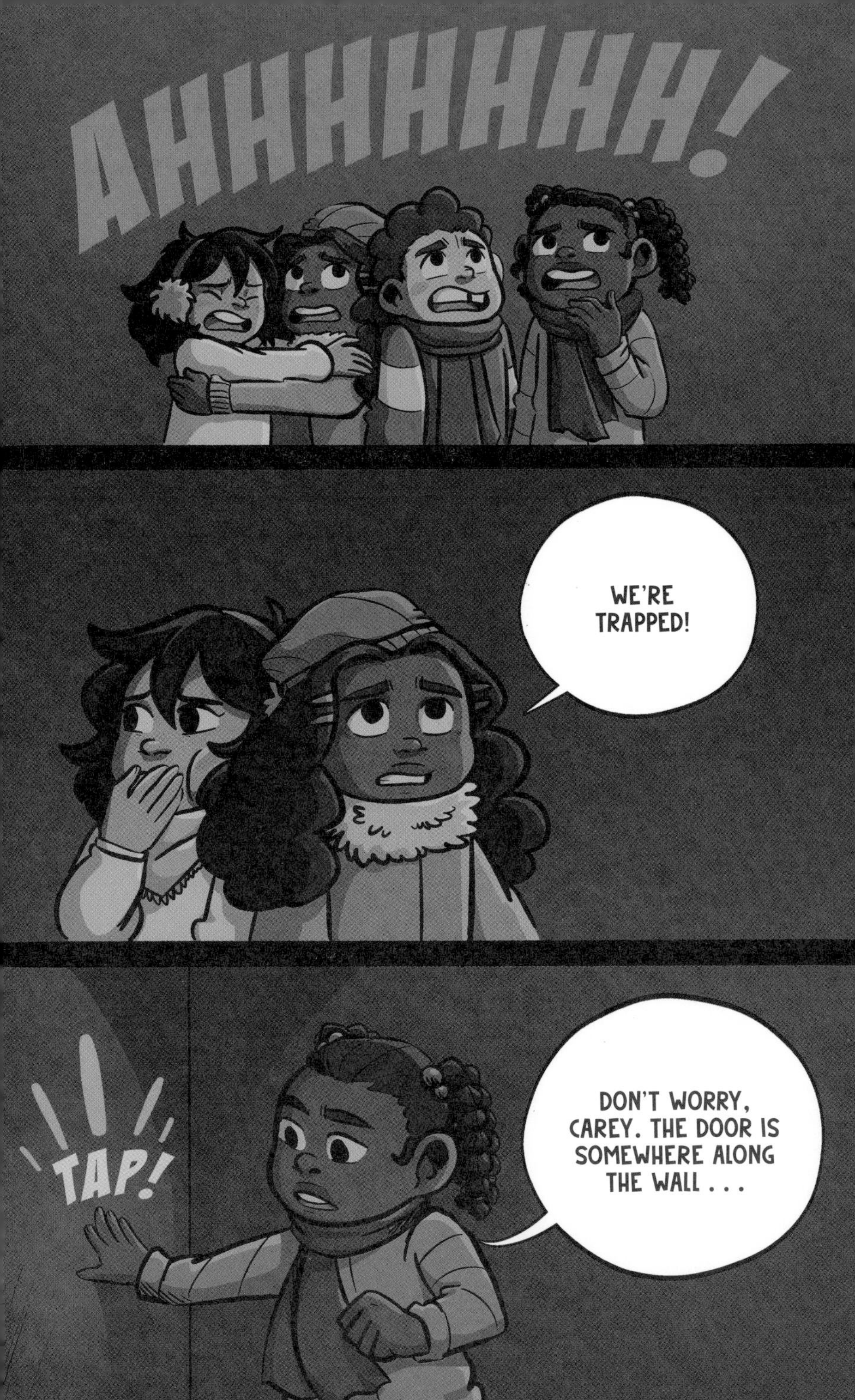
AHHHHHHH!
WE'RE TRAPPED!
TAP!
DON'T WORRY, CAREY. THE DOOR IS SOMEWHERE ALONG THE WALL . . .

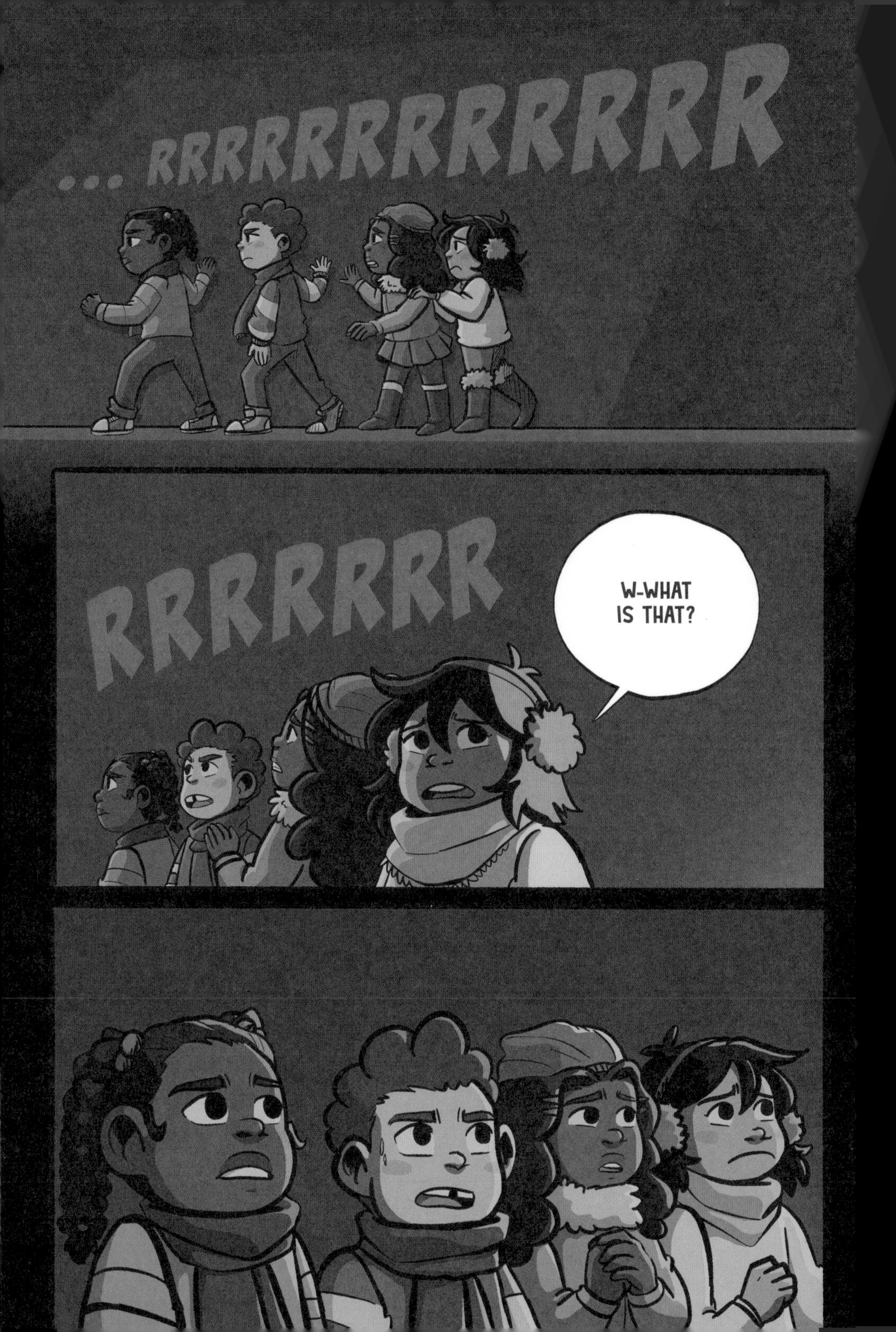
...RRRRRRRRRRRRR
RRRRRRR
W-WHAT IS THAT?

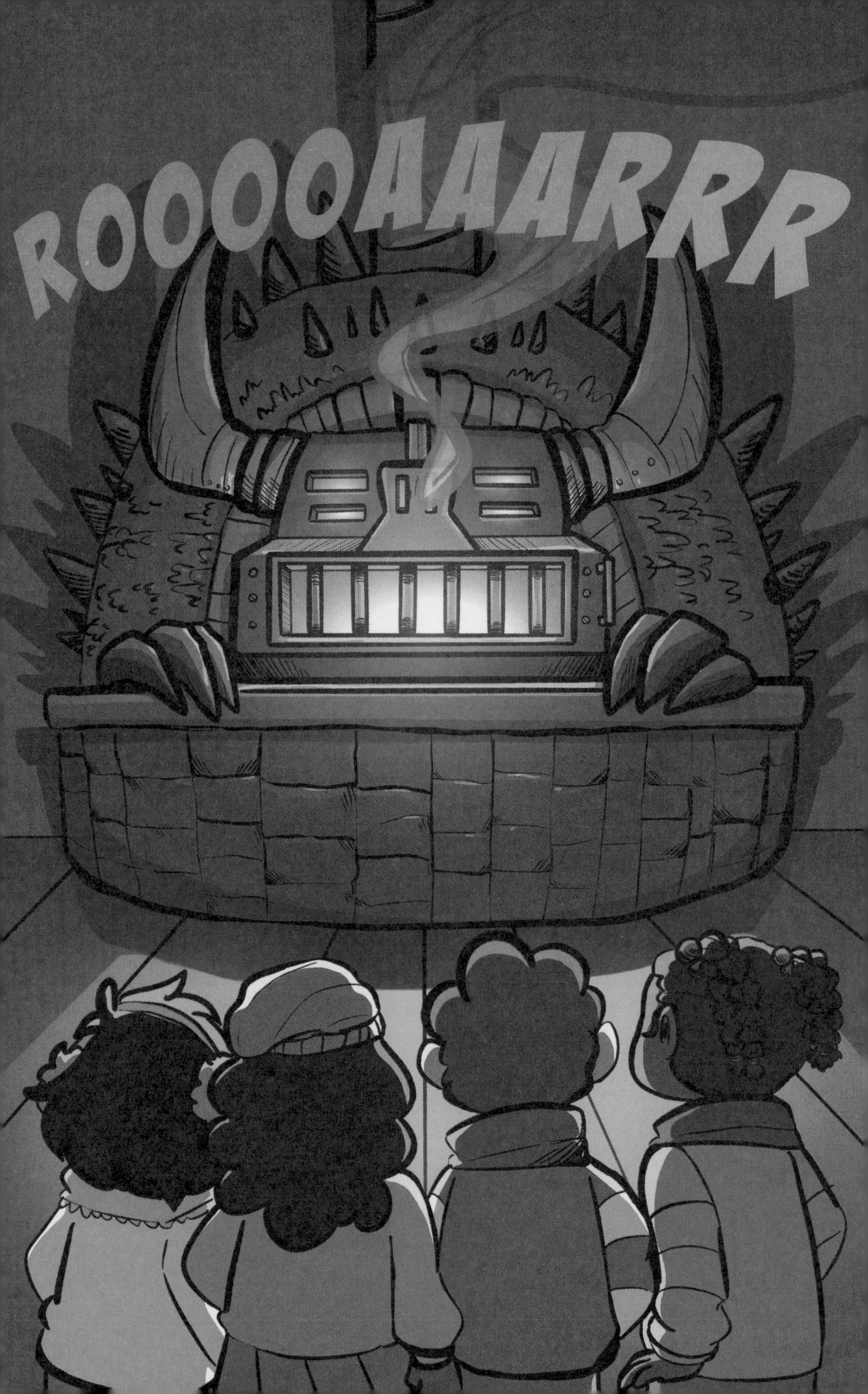
ROOOOAAARRR

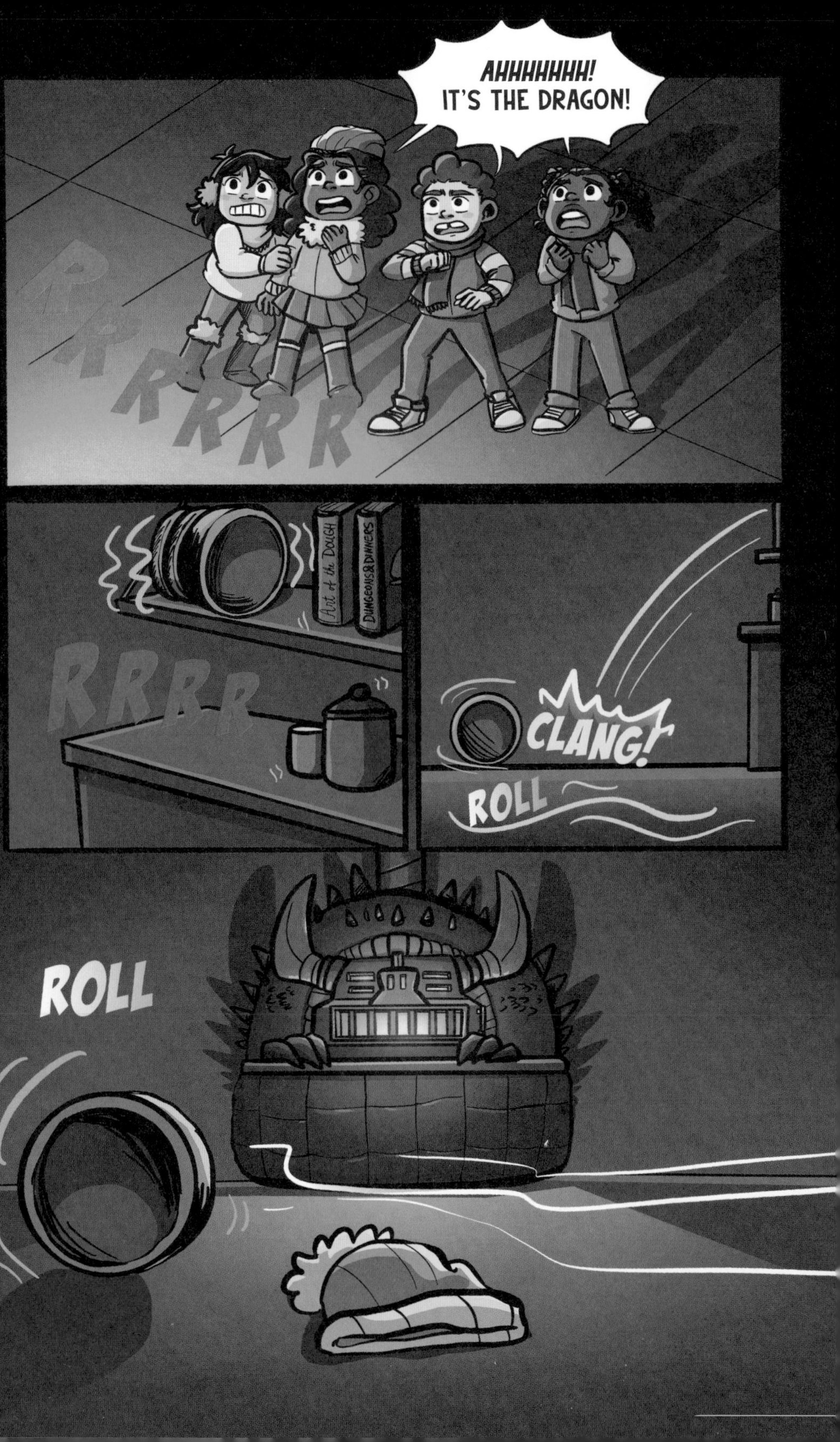
AHHHHHHH!
IT'S THE DRAGON!
RRRRRRR
Art of the DOUGH
DUNGEONS & DINNERS
RRRR
CLANG!
ROLL
ROLL

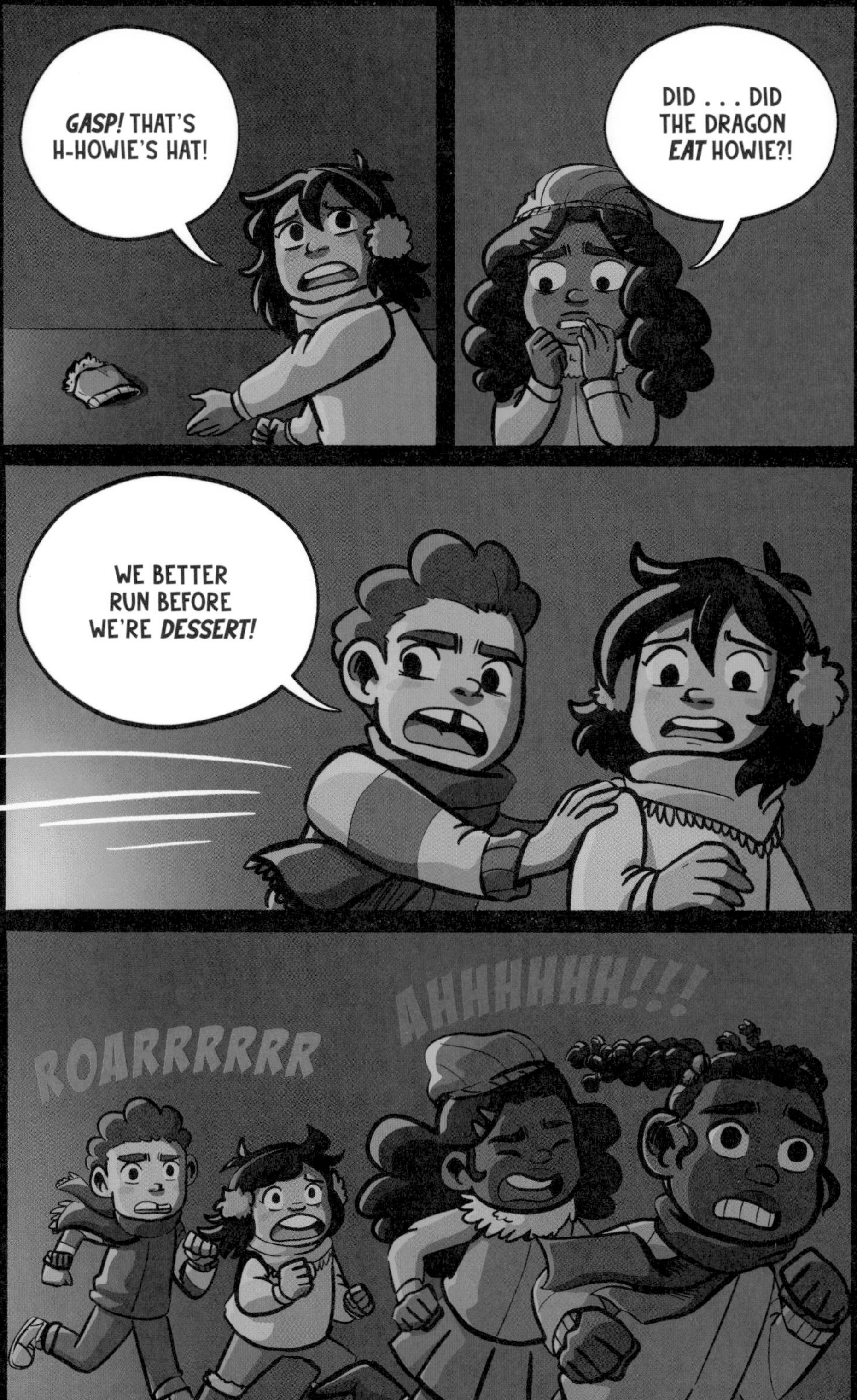
GASP! THAT'S H-HOWIE'S HAT!
DID . . . DID THE DRAGON EAT HOWIE?!
WE BETTER RUN BEFORE WE'RE DESSERT!
ROARRRRRR
AHHHHHH!!!

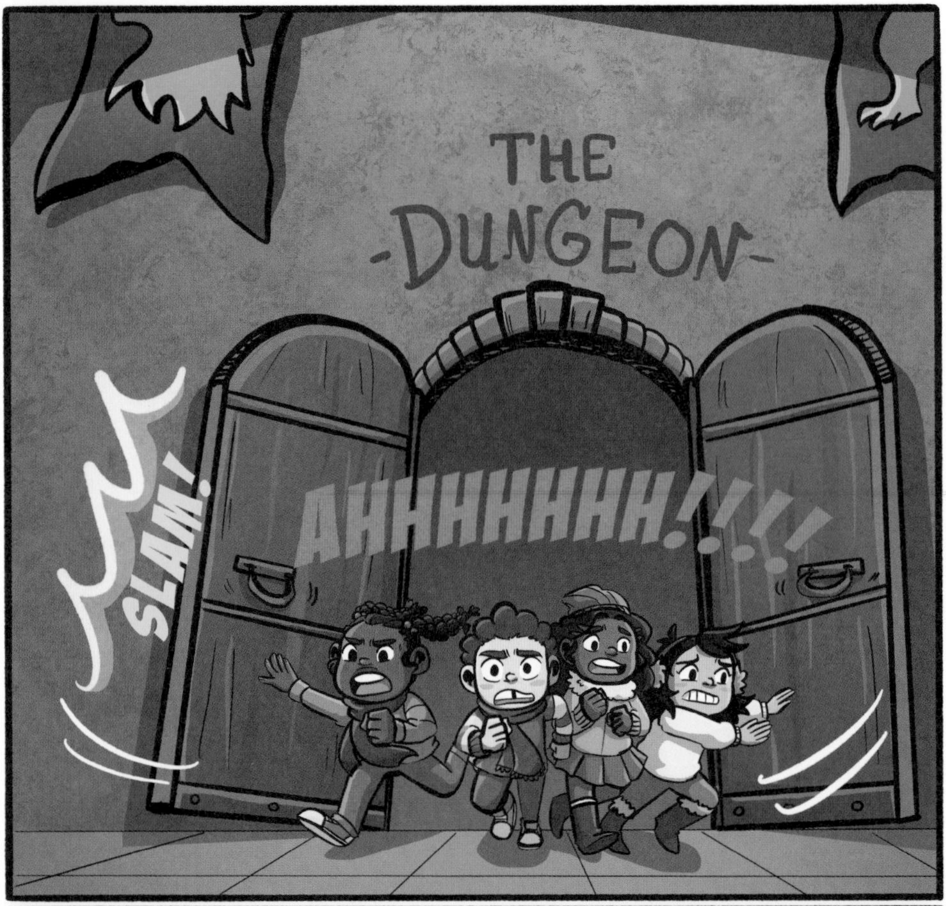
THE
-DUNGEON-
SLAM!
AHHHHHHH!!!!

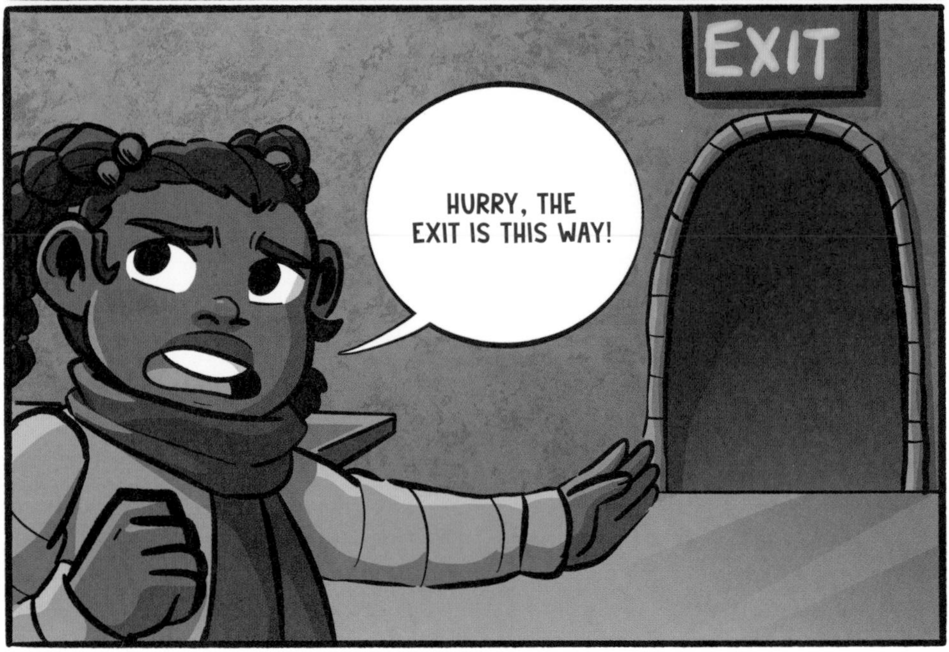
EXIT
HURRY, THE
EXIT IS THIS WAY!

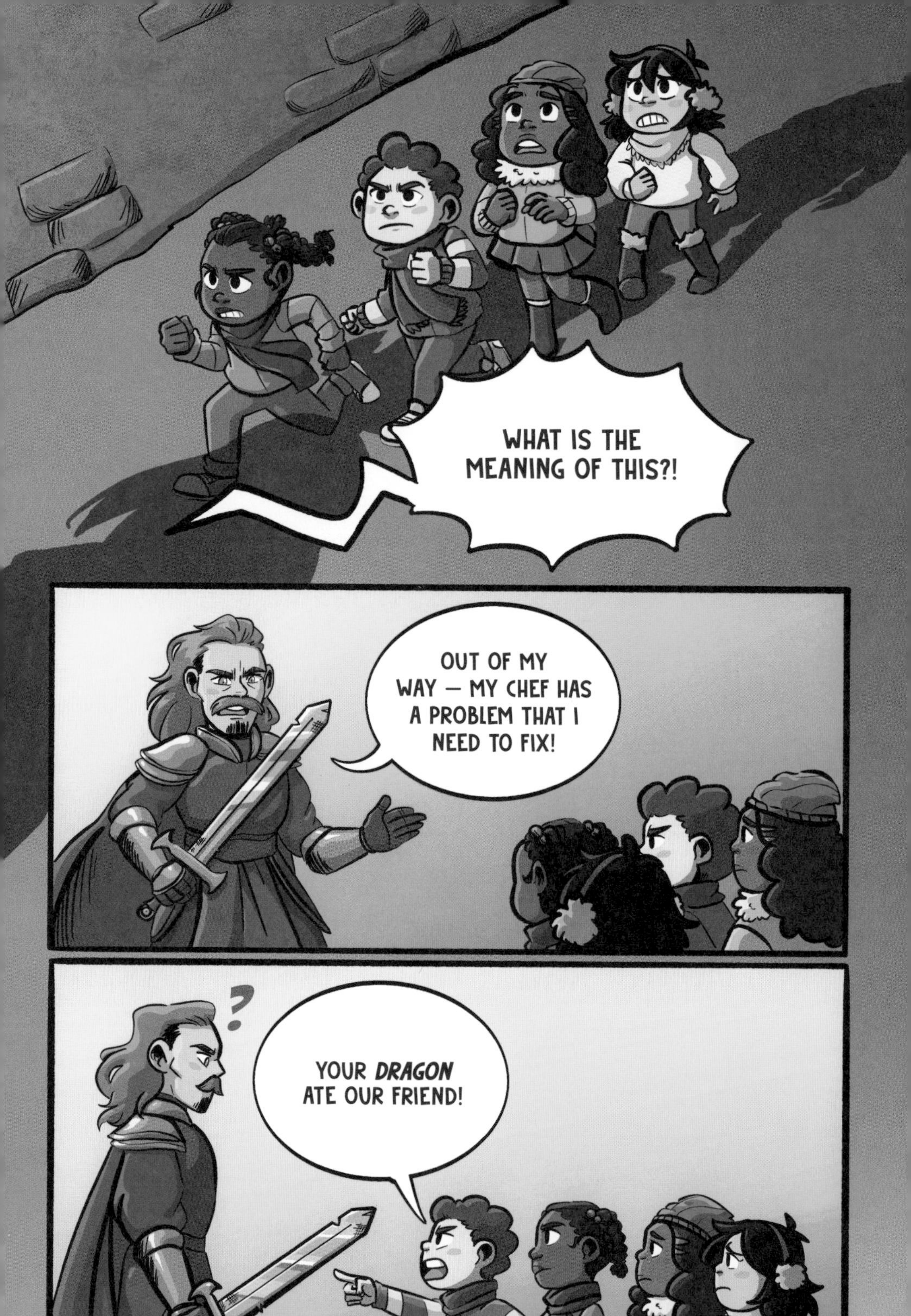
WHAT IS THE MEANING OF THIS?!
OUT OF MY WAY — MY CHEF HAS A PROBLEM THAT I NEED TO FIX!
?
YOUR *DRAGON* ATE OUR FRIEND!

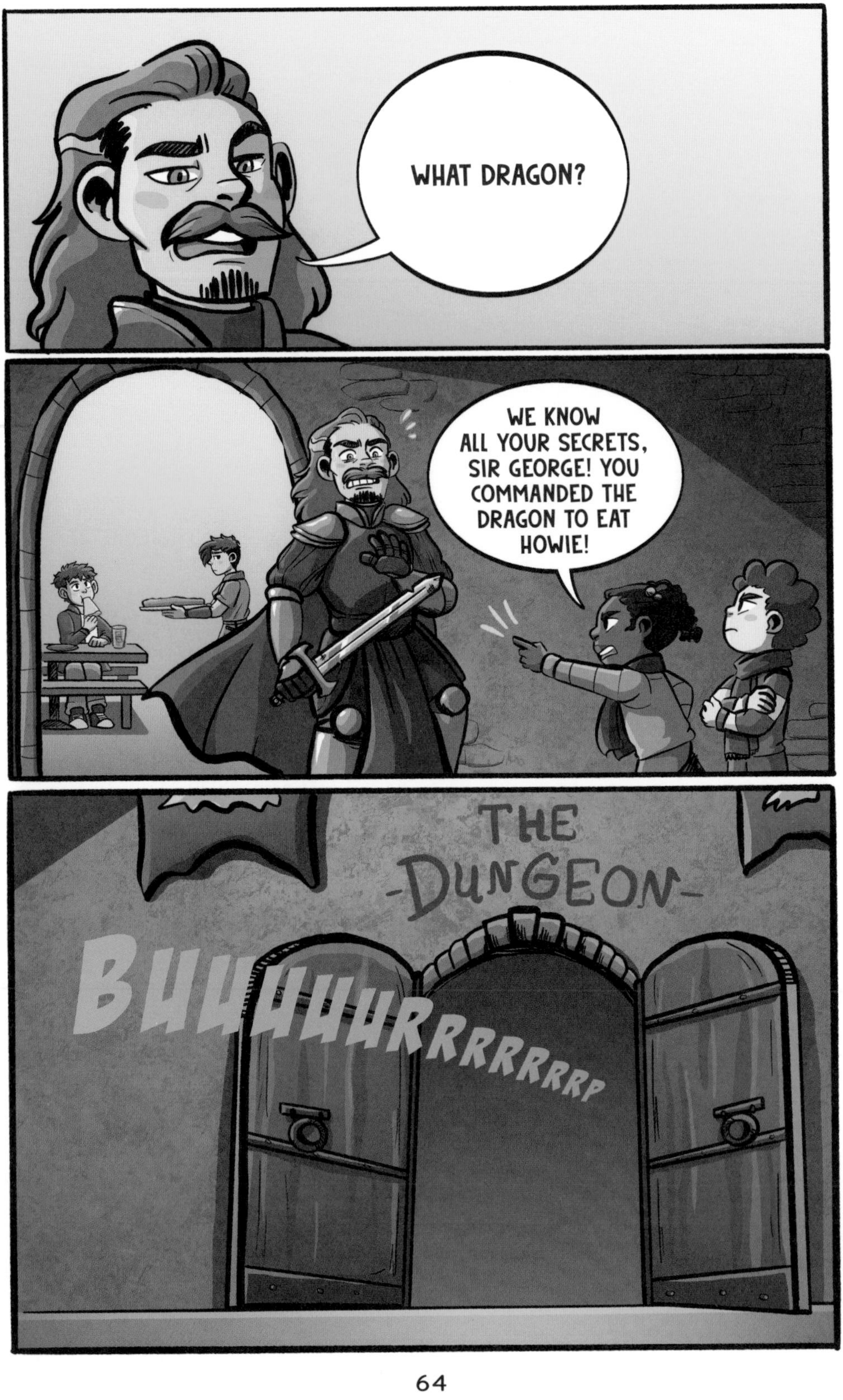
WHAT DRAGON?
WE KNOW ALL YOUR SECRETS, SIR GEORGE! YOU COMMANDED THE DRAGON TO EAT HOWIE!
THE DUNGEON
BUUUUUURRRRRRRP

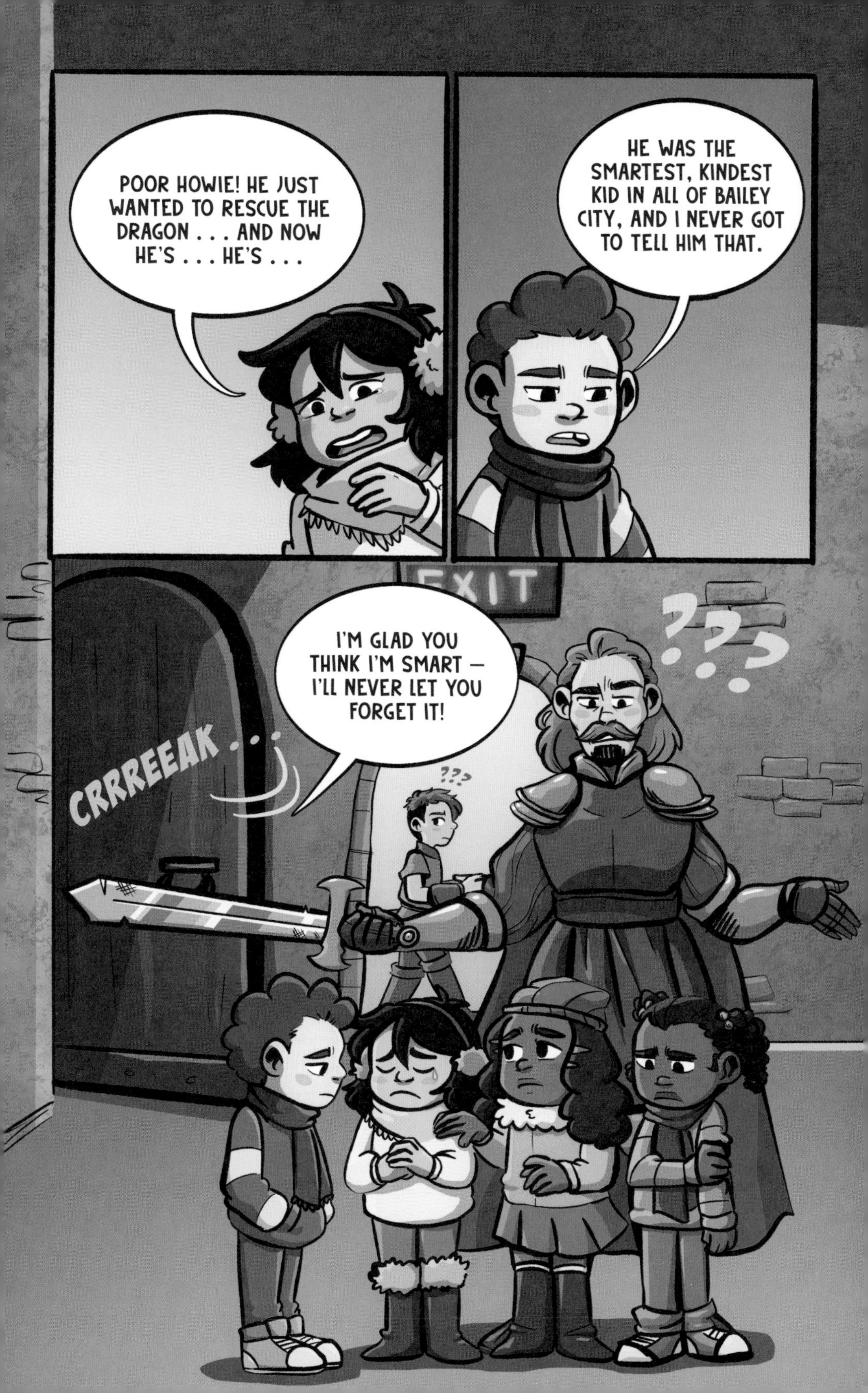
POOR HOWIE! HE JUST WANTED TO RESCUE THE DRAGON . . . AND NOW HE'S . . . HE'S . . .
HE WAS THE SMARTEST, KINDEST KID IN ALL OF BAILEY CITY, AND I NEVER GOT TO TELL HIM THAT.
EXIT
CRRREEAK . . .
I'M GLAD YOU THINK I'M SMART — I'LL NEVER LET YOU FORGET IT!
???
???

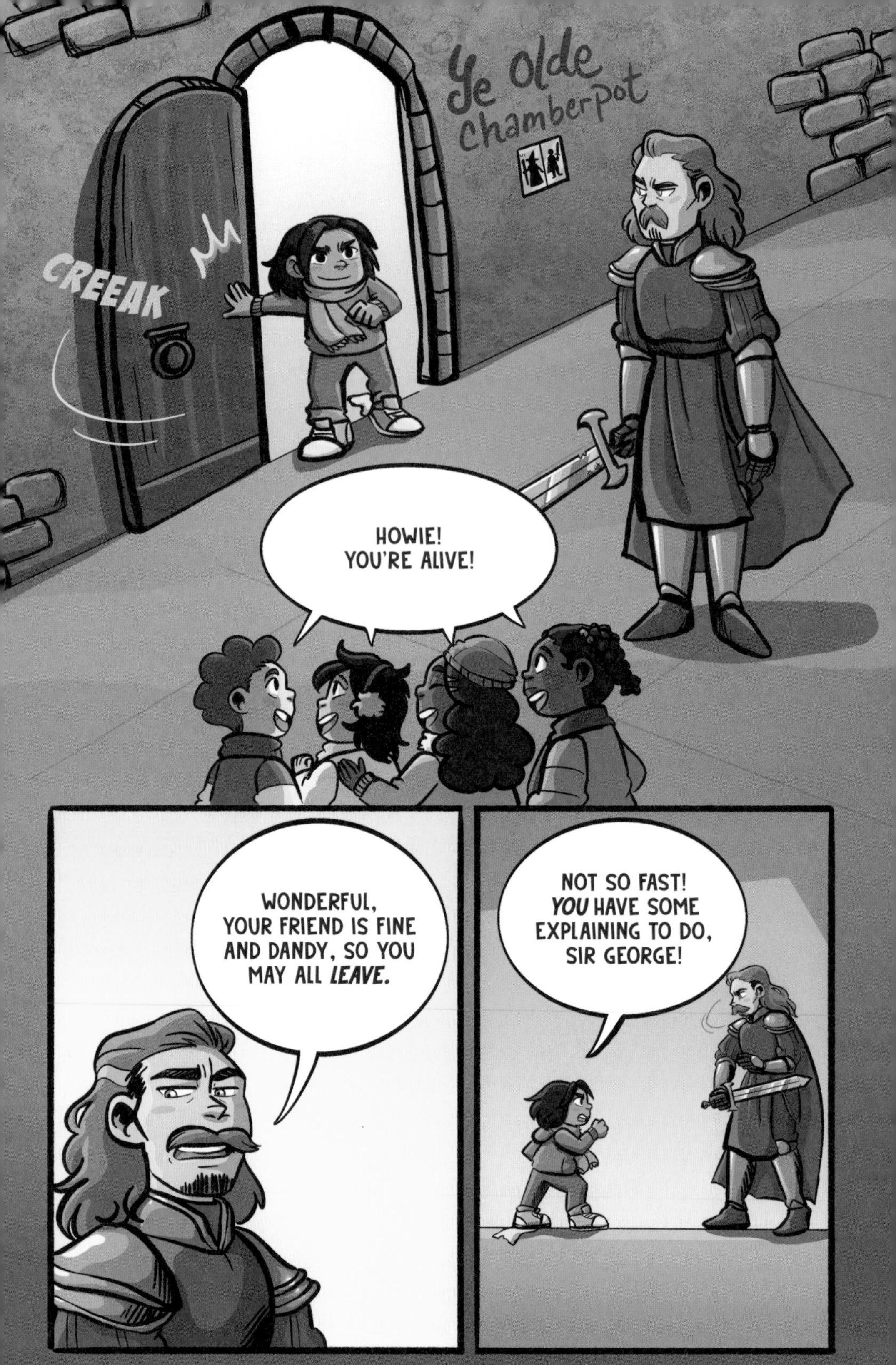
Ye Olde Chamberpot
CREEAK
HOWIE! YOU'RE ALIVE!
WONDERFUL, YOUR FRIEND IS FINE AND DANDY, SO YOU MAY ALL *LEAVE.*
NOT SO FAST! *YOU* HAVE SOME EXPLAINING TO DO, SIR GEORGE!

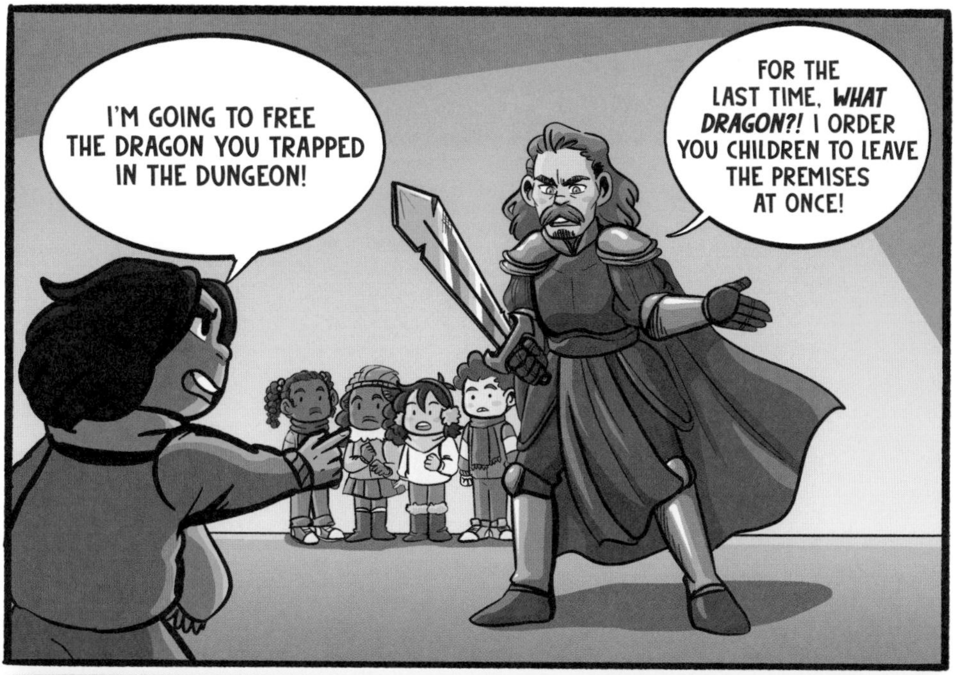
I'M GOING TO FREE THE DRAGON YOU TRAPPED IN THE DUNGEON!
FOR THE LAST TIME, **WHAT DRAGON?!** I ORDER YOU CHILDREN TO LEAVE THE PREMISES AT ONCE!

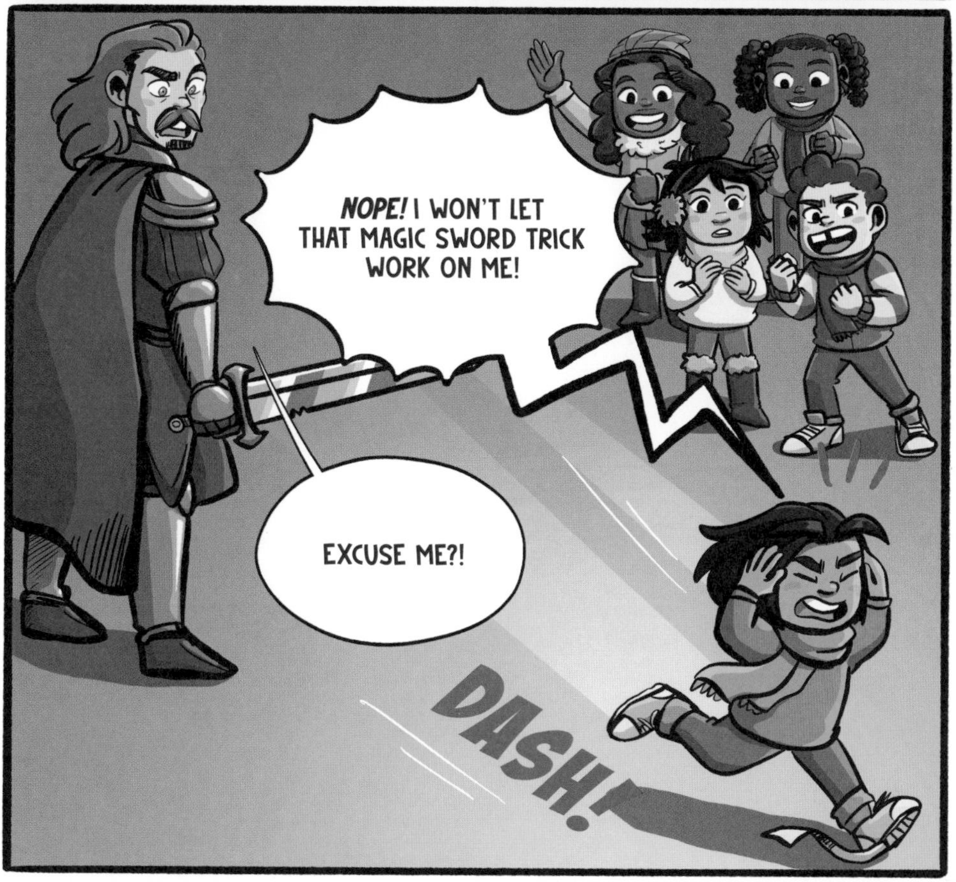
NOPE! I WON'T LET THAT MAGIC SWORD TRICK WORK ON ME!
EXCUSE ME?!
DASH!

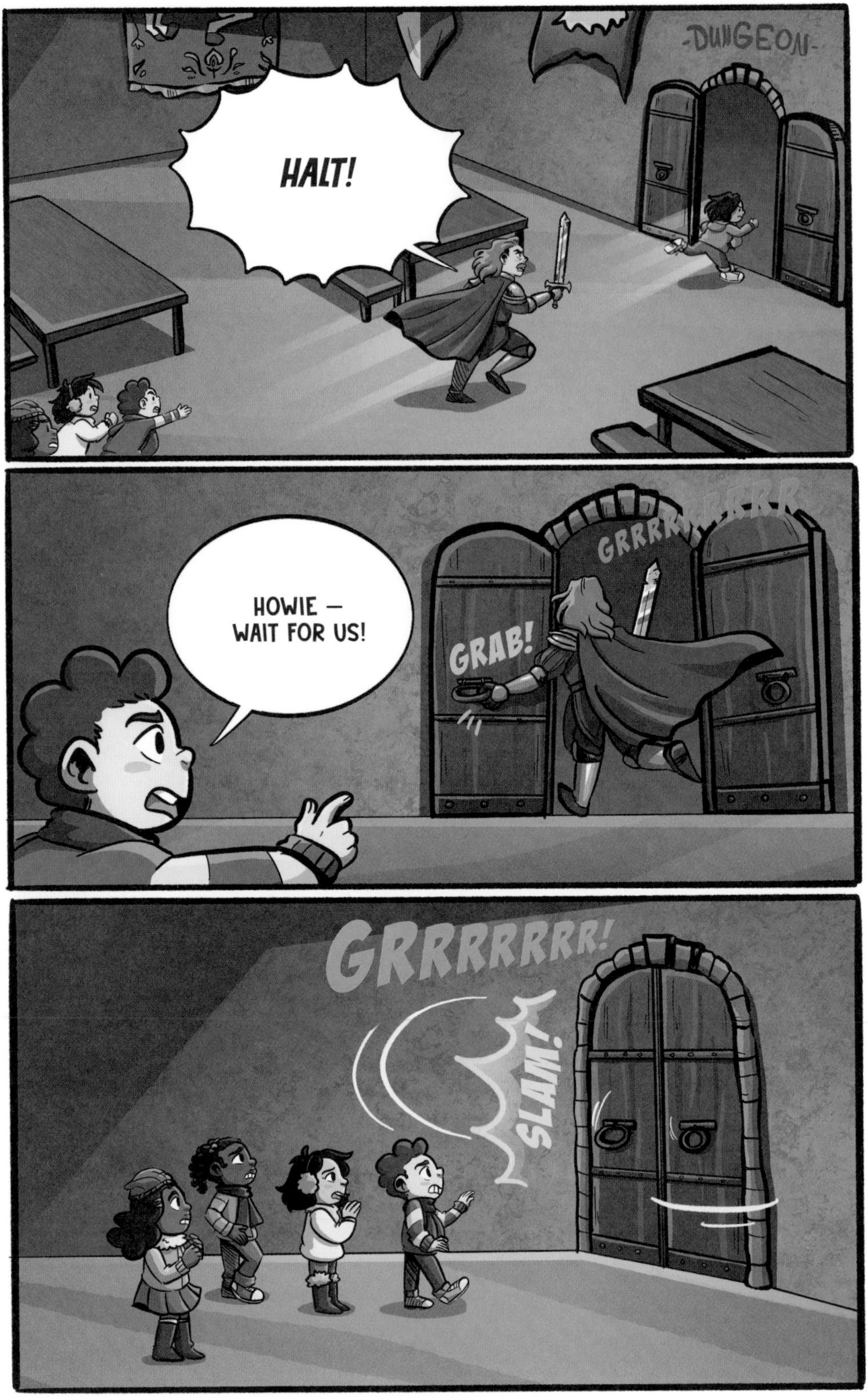

-DUNGEON-
HALT!
HOWIE — WAIT FOR US!
GRAB!
GRRRRRRRR
GRRRRRRR!
SLAM!

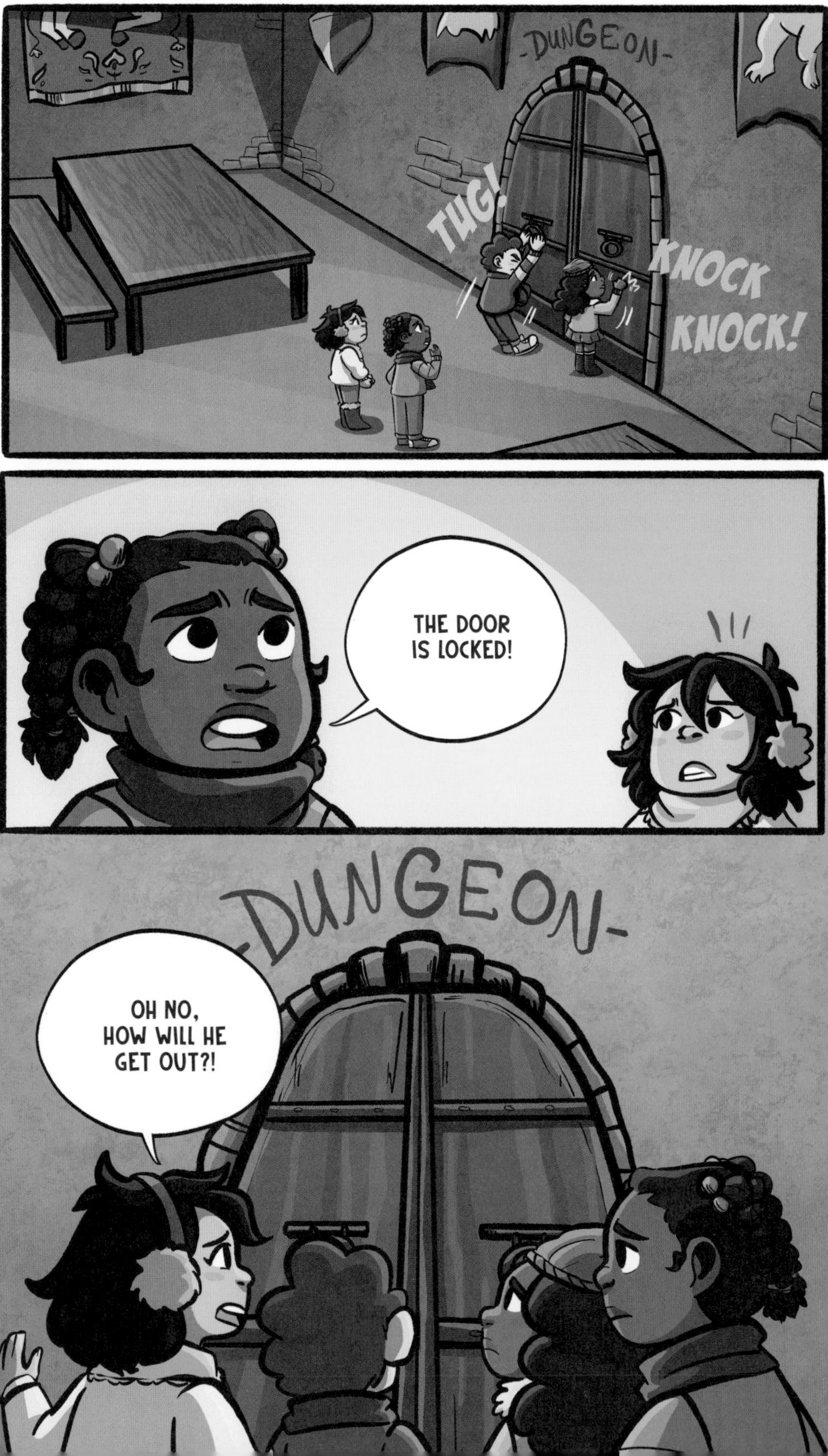
-DUNGEON-
TUG!
KNOCK KNOCK!
THE DOOR IS LOCKED!
-DUNGEON-
OH NO, HOW WILL HE GET OUT?!

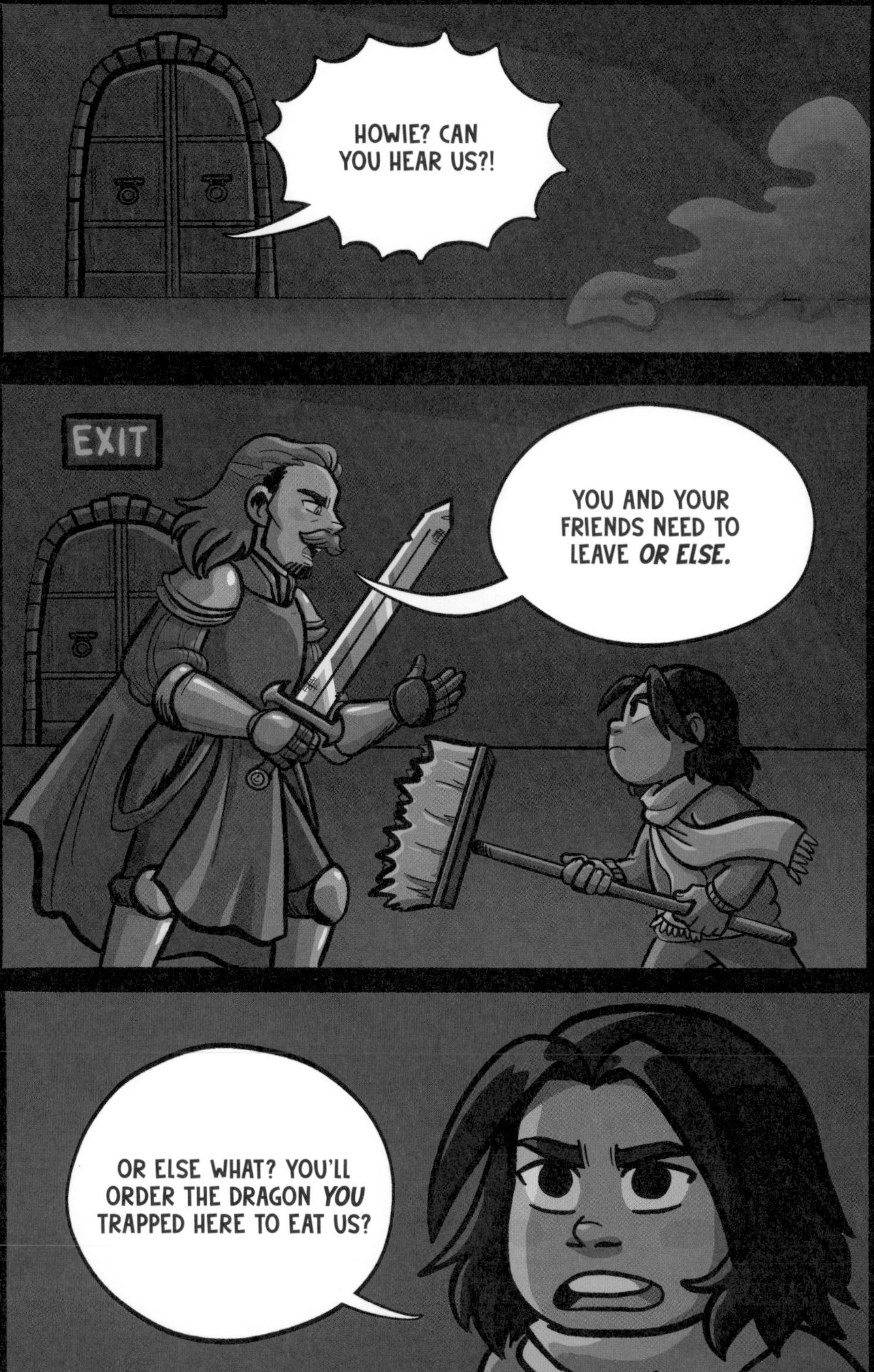
HOWIE? CAN YOU HEAR US?!
EXIT
YOU AND YOUR FRIENDS NEED TO LEAVE *OR ELSE.*
OR ELSE WHAT? YOU'LL ORDER THE DRAGON *YOU* TRAPPED HERE TO EAT US?

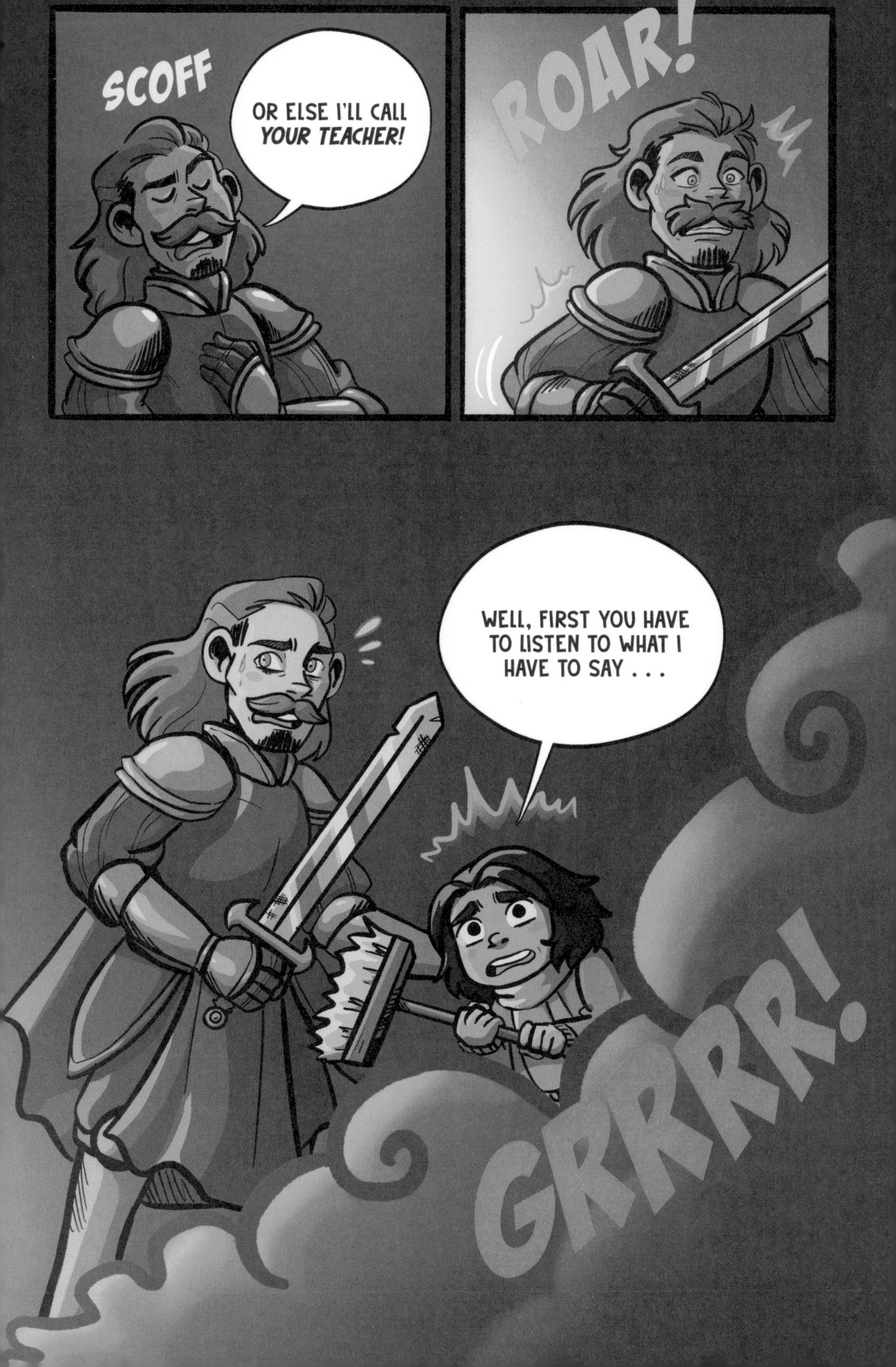
SCOFF
OR ELSE I'LL CALL YOUR TEACHER!
ROAR!
WELL, FIRST YOU HAVE TO LISTEN TO WHAT I HAVE TO SAY . . .
GRRRR!

CHAPTER 5 GRAND REOPENING

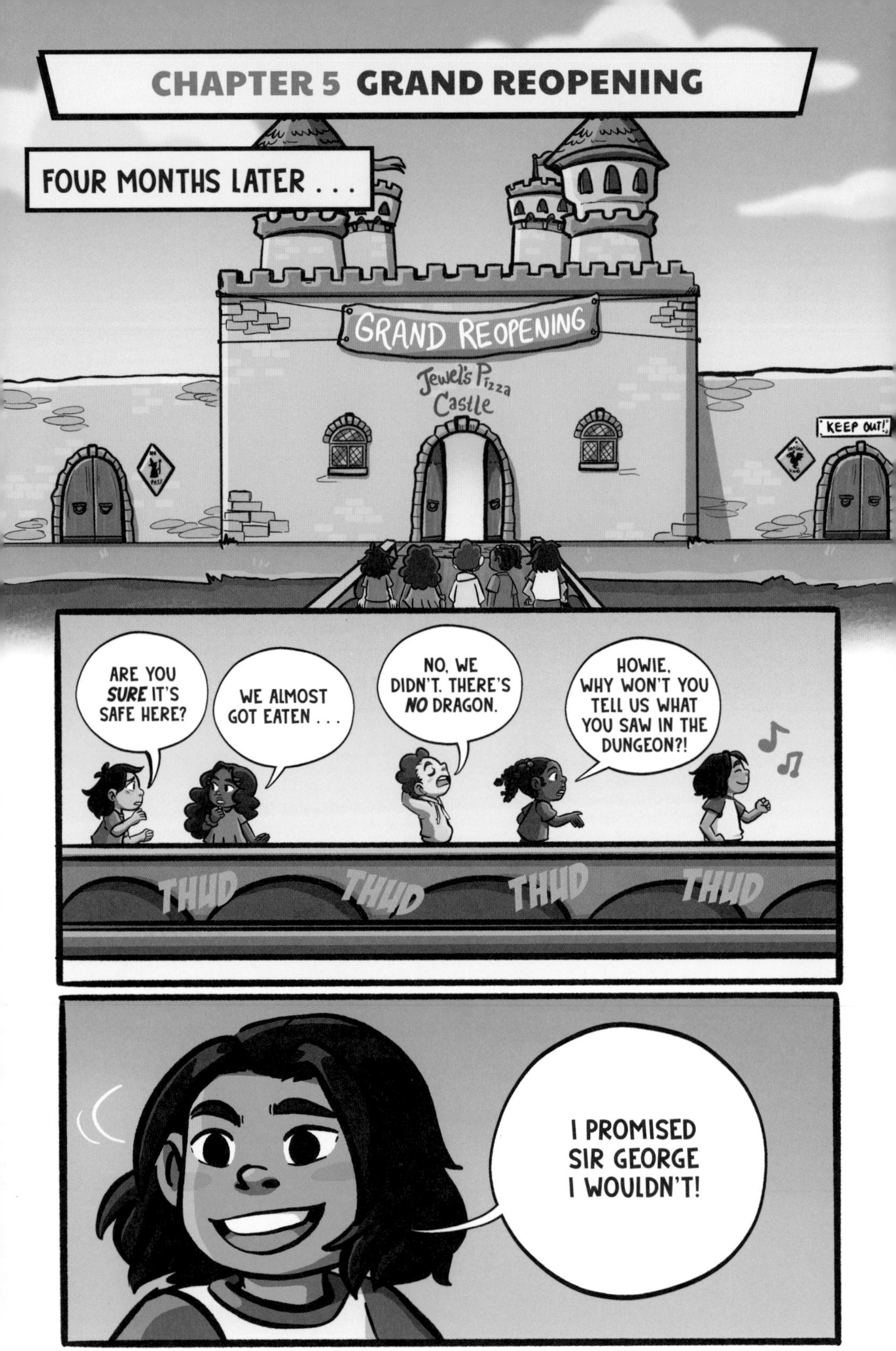
FOUR MONTHS LATER . . .
GRAND REOPENING
Jewel's Pizza Castle
KEEP OUT!
ARE YOU *SURE* IT'S SAFE HERE?
WE ALMOST GOT EATEN . . .
NO, WE DIDN'T. THERE'S *NO* DRAGON.
HOWIE, WHY WON'T YOU TELL US WHAT YOU SAW IN THE DUNGEON?!
THUD THUD THUD THUD
I PROMISED SIR GEORGE I WOULDN'T!

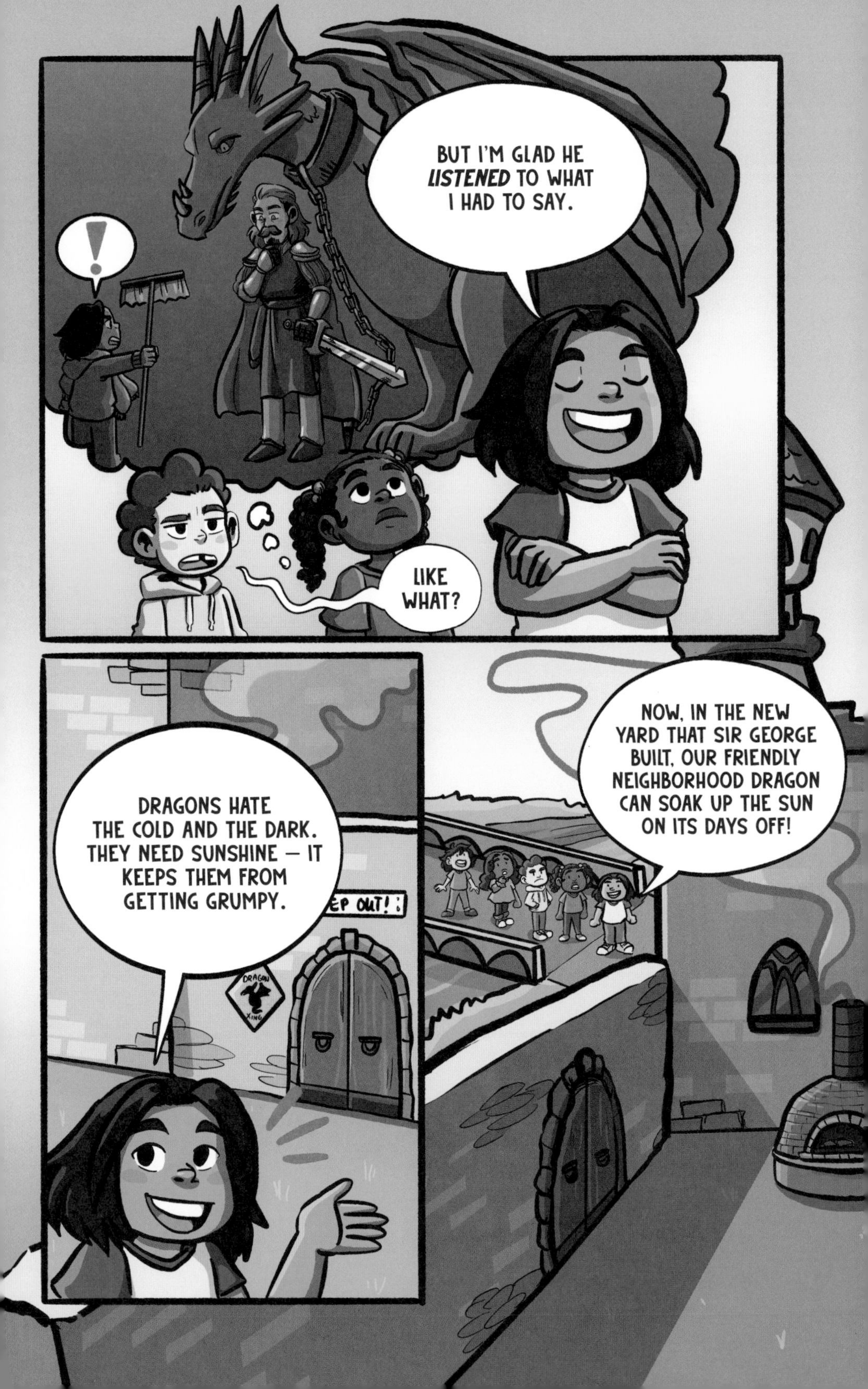
!
BUT I'M GLAD HE *LISTENED* TO WHAT I HAD TO SAY.
LIKE WHAT?
DRAGONS HATE THE COLD AND THE DARK. THEY NEED SUNSHINE — IT KEEPS THEM FROM GETTING GRUMPY.
NOW, IN THE NEW YARD THAT SIR GEORGE BUILT, OUR FRIENDLY NEIGHBORHOOD DRAGON CAN SOAK UP THE SUN ON ITS DAYS OFF!
EP OUT!

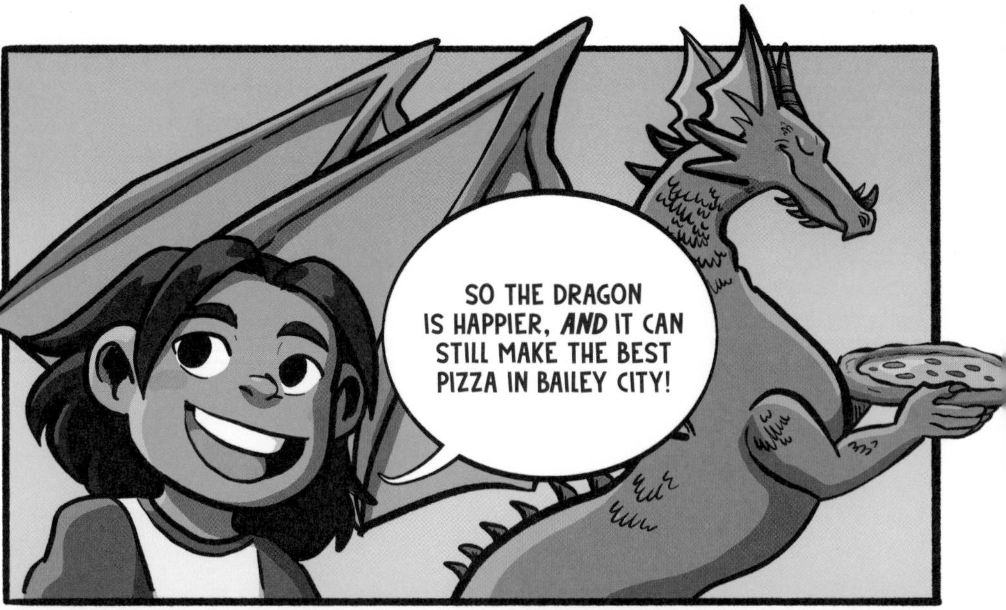
SO THE DRAGON IS HAPPIER, *AND* IT CAN STILL MAKE THE BEST PIZZA IN BAILEY CITY!

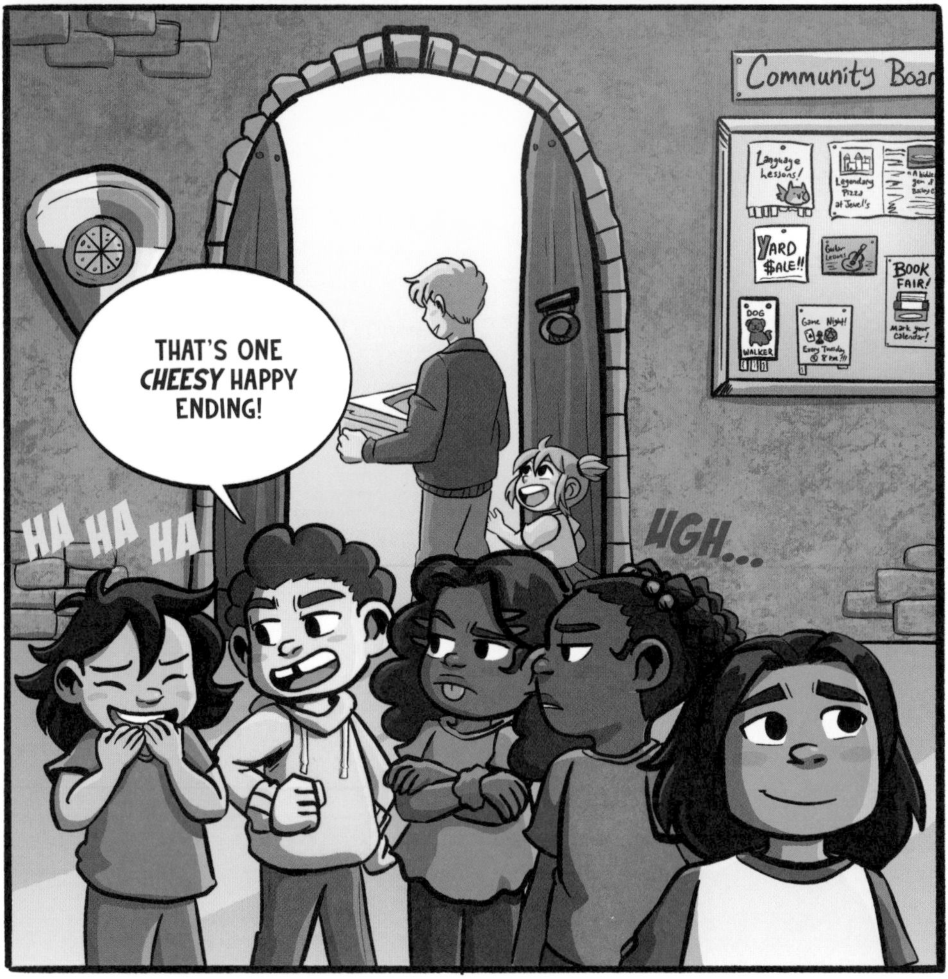
YARD $ALE!!
BOOK FAIR!
DOG WALKER
THAT'S ONE *CHEESY* HAPPY ENDING!
HA HA HA
UGH...

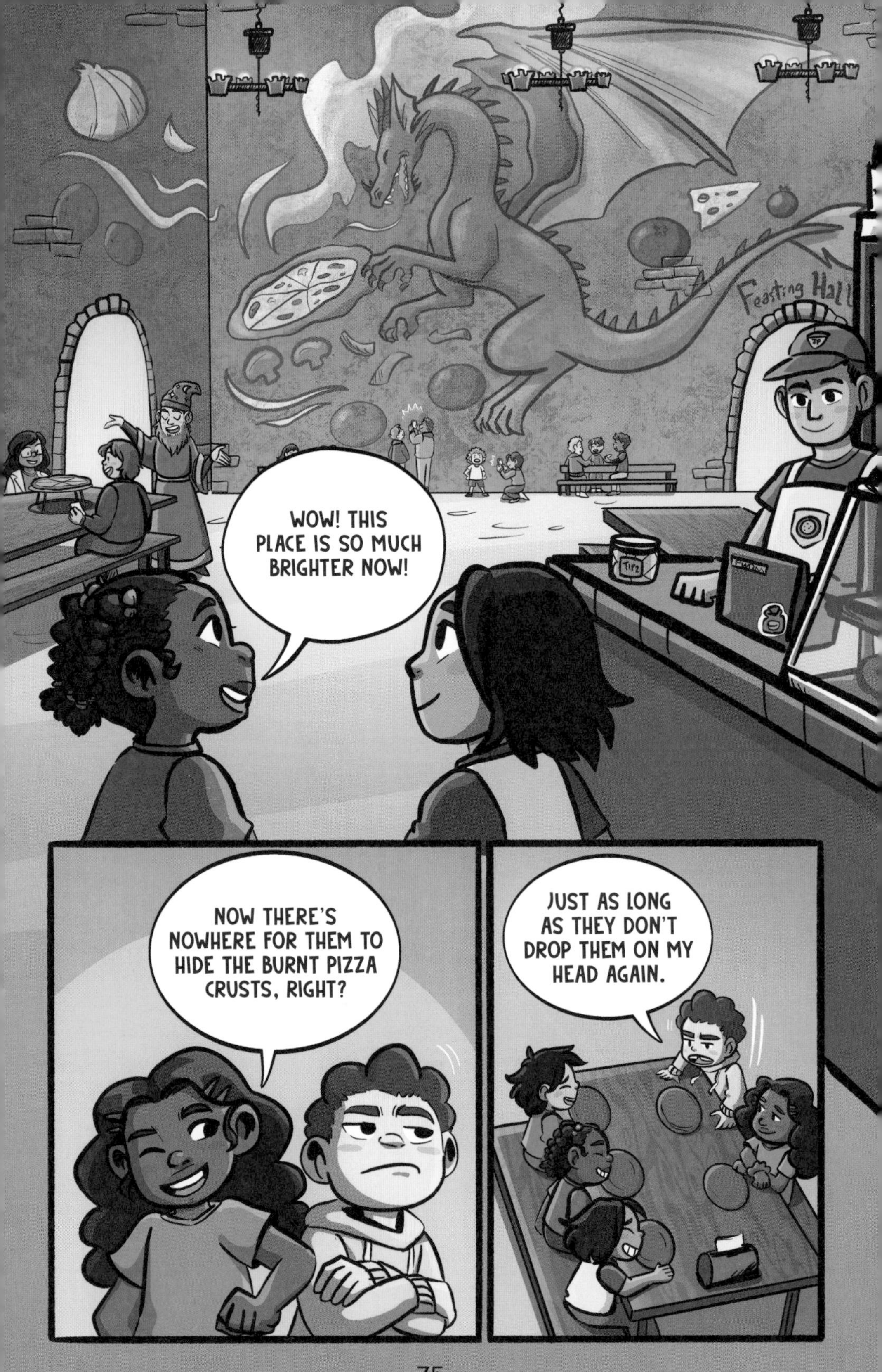
WOW! THIS PLACE IS SO MUCH BRIGHTER NOW!
NOW THERE'S NOWHERE FOR THEM TO HIDE THE BURNT PIZZA CRUSTS, RIGHT?
JUST AS LONG AS THEY DON'T DROP THEM ON MY HEAD AGAIN.

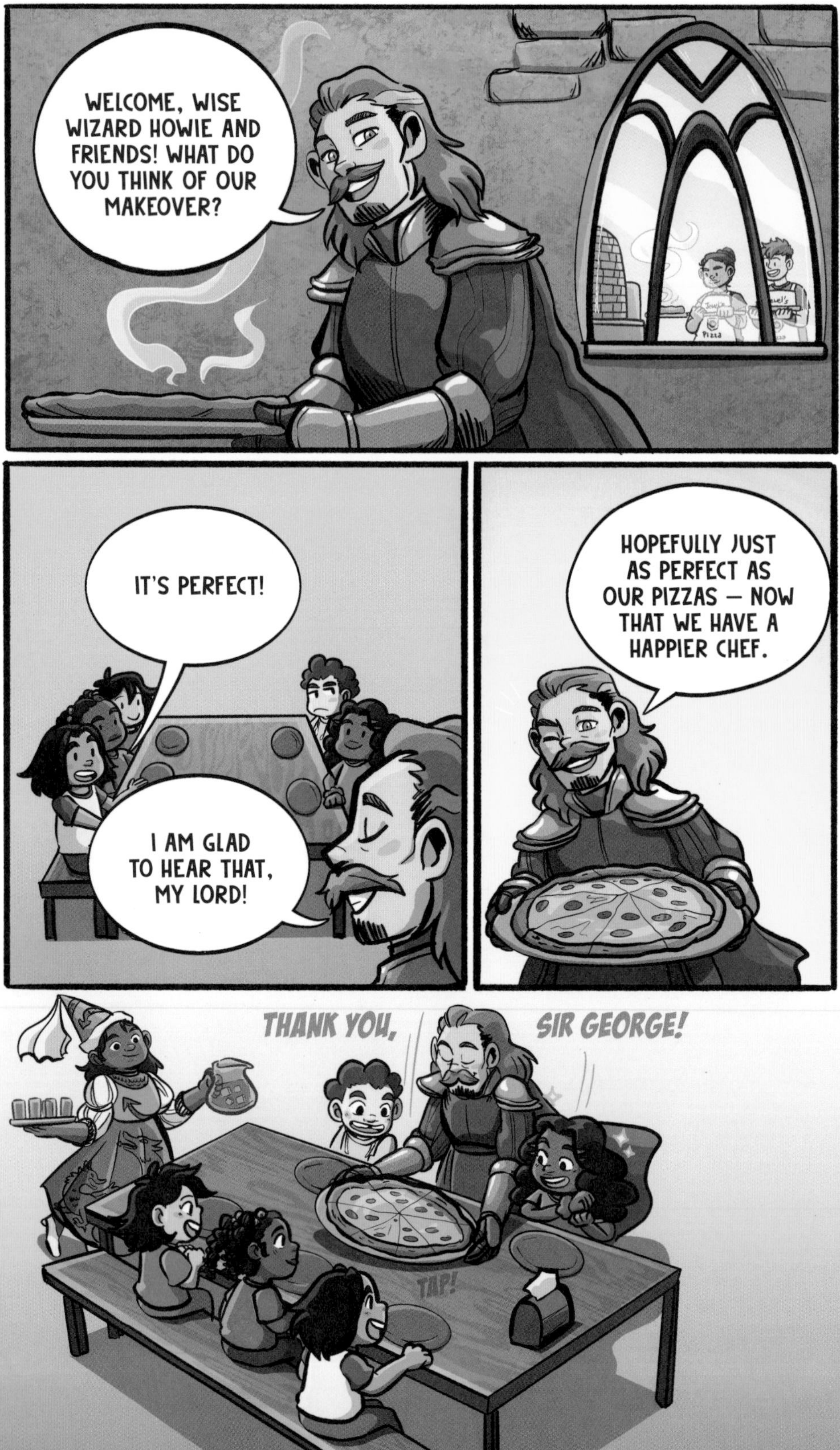
WELCOME, WISE WIZARD HOWIE AND FRIENDS! WHAT DO YOU THINK OF OUR MAKEOVER?
IT'S PERFECT!
I AM GLAD TO HEAR THAT, MY LORD!
HOPEFULLY JUST AS PERFECT AS OUR PIZZAS — NOW THAT WE HAVE A HAPPIER CHEF.
THANK YOU,
SIR GEORGE!
TAP!

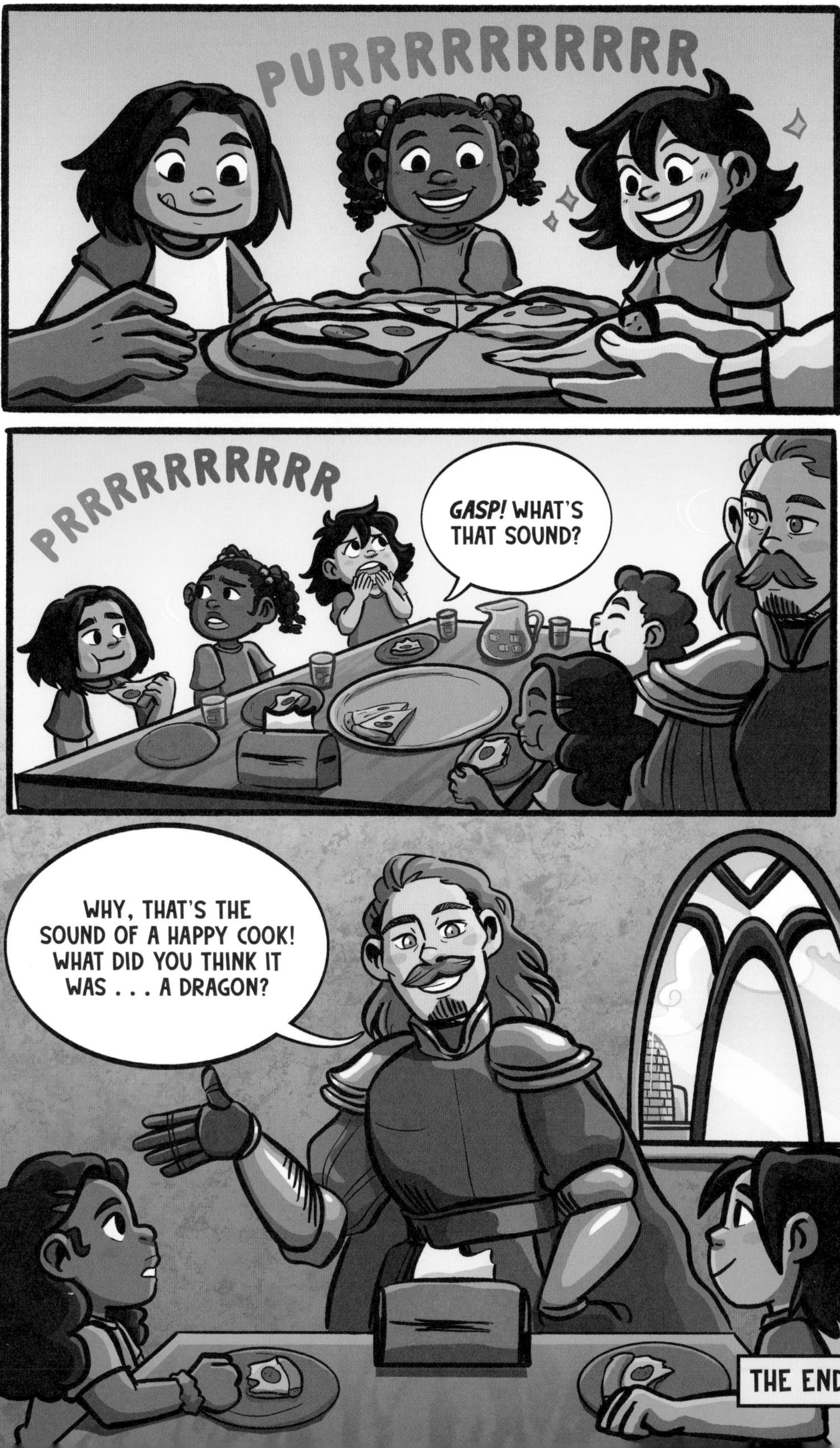
PURRRRRRRRRR
PRRRRRRRRRR
GASP! WHAT'S THAT SOUND?
WHY, THAT'S THE SOUND OF A HAPPY COOK! WHAT DID YOU THINK IT WAS . . . A DRAGON?
THE END

MARCIA THORNTON JONES is an award-winning author who has published more than 135 books for children, including the Adventures of the Bailey School Kids series, *Woodford Brave*, *Ratfink*, and *Champ*. Marcia lives with her husband, Steve, and two cats in Lexington, Kentucky, where she mentors and teaches writing.

DEBBIE DADEY grew up in Kentucky and now lives in New Hampshire with her husband and two rescue greyhounds. Her three adult children continue to inspire her. A former first-grade teacher and school librarian, she is the author and coauthor of 182 books, including the Adventures of the Bailey School Kids series. Her newest series, Mini Mermaid Tales, is a multicultural easy chapter book series from Simon and Schuster. Her newest picture book is *Never Give Up: Dr. Kati Karikó and the Race for the Future of Vaccines*.

ANGELI RAFER is a Filipino American illustrator and comic artist based in the diner capital of the world (a.k.a. New Jersey). She is a self-taught digital artist with a passion for telling stories about everyday magic — from cooking and first crushes to cute animals and bad puns. For more of her work featuring the Bailey School Kids, check out her 2023 Graphix Chapters book: *Ghosts Don't Eat Potato Chips!*